Winnie
The Horse Gentler

6

Tyndale House Publishers, Inc.
Carol Stream, Illinois

Gift Horse

DANDI DALEY MACKALL

Visit Tyndale's exciting Web site at www.tyndale.com

Visit the exciting Web site for kids at www.cool2read.com and the Winnie the Horse Gentler Web site at www.winniethehorsegentler.com

You can contact Dandi Daley Mackall through her Web site at www.dandibooks.com

Tyndale Kids logo is a trademark of Tyndale House Publishers, Inc.

Gift Horse

Designed by Jacqueline Noe

Edited by Ramona Cramer Tucker

This novel is a work of fiction. Names, characters, places, and incidents either are the product of the author's imagination or are used fictitiously. Any resemblance to actual events, locales, organizations, or persons, living or dead, is entirely coincidental and beyond the intent of either the author or publisher.

ISBN-13: 978-0-8423-5547-6, mass paper
ISBN-10: 0-8423-5547-2, mass paper

Printed in the United States of America

13 12 11 10 09 08 07
10 9   8   7   6   5   4

*To Mrs. Gorton
and Mr. Hatt,
gifted teachers*

I watched as my buddy Hawk, a.k.a. Victoria Hawkins to her popular friends, led Towaco, her Appaloosa, out of my barn. Frost puffed from his nostrils. Snow dusted Hawk's dad's new trailer.

"Load him up!" Mr. Hawkins called.

I wanted to grab Hawk and Towaco and gallop out of there at Thoroughbred speed.

Near the trailer my dad and his *friend* and fellow inventor, Madeline Edison, watched. Actually, they were watching Madeline's seven-year-old son watching the Appaloosa. Mason has a condition that makes him unplug the world sometimes and tune everybody out. But he'd bonded with Towaco when I'd given him riding lessons and a special kind of horse therapy. Madeline wanted him to see the Appy off.

Mr. Hawkins, in dress pants and a gray over-coat, was keeping his distance from horsehair. Hawk's parents were in the middle of a divorce, and her dad was moving to Florida. Hawk said he'd taken a partnership in a law office, where he'd be defending murderers and robbers. She got to miss the next week and a half of school to go with him to see his new place. Plus, her dad had entered Towaco in a Florida horse show.

"I will be back before New Year's," Hawk promised as we reached the trailer. "Do not look so sad."

I tried to grin back at her. True, I'd miss Hawk. It had taken us months to become good friends. But that wasn't what had my stomach knotted like a hobbled stallion. I watched the snowflakes layer white on Hawk's long, dark hair. Tiny drifts pressed against the trailer tires.

"Mr. Hawkins?" My voice, which always sounds gravelly, cracked. "Maybe you should wait until the snowstorm's over."

He laughed. His perfect haircut didn't budge in the wind. "This is hardly a snowstorm, Winifred. At any rate, we'll drive out of it."

"But the roads. They'll be slick. And with the trailer—," I started.

Dad stopped me. "They'll be all right, Winnie." His eyes looked sad, and I knew he knew.

I was remembering a blizzard in Wyoming two years ago, the day Mom and I had gone out in it to see a horse. My mind flashed a picture of the instant after our car spun on the ice and out of control. I have a photographic memory—not a *good* memory, but one that stores pictures in my brain and spits them out, even when I don't want to see them. And I didn't want to see this one—my mom's hand limp over the steering wheel, her head against the window. . . .

Nickers, my white Arabian, whinnied from the paddock. She pranced along the fence, looking gorgeous, as white as the snow falling around her. Sometimes I think she knows exactly what I'm thinking and exactly what I need.

"Nickers doesn't want you to go either, Hawk," I said, pretending that's all there was to it. "She'll miss Towaco."

Towaco had been my first "problem horse" when I set up business as Winnie the Horse Gentler in Ashland, Ohio. I'm only in seventh grade, but I learned from the best, my mom. She *gentled* horses instead of breaking them. And now people pay me to do the same thing.

"Towaco!" Mason let out the name like a cry from his soul. It hurt to hear it. Pulling away from his mom, he ran up to the Appy. His stocking cap flew off, and wisps of angel-blond hair blew across his forehead. Green mittens reached up for Towaco's neck.

Hawk lifted him so he could hug her horse. Mason's lighter than a sack of feed. "Towaco is coming back, Mason," Hawk promised. "Maybe he will bring you back a blue ribbon from the Florida horse show. Wouldn't that be nice?"

Mason's little shoulders shook when Hawk set him down. "Don't go, Towaco," he whispered.

Towaco nuzzled Mason's hair. Mason hardly talked at all around us until he and Towaco got so close.

"They'll be back, Mason," I said, kneeling beside him.

But he didn't seem to hear me. He stared, unblinking, at a spot on Towaco's shoulder. He'd already gone away in his mind.

Madeline walked up and put her hands on Mason's shoulders. "Come on, honey," she coaxed, drawing him away from the Appy.

"Hey, tiger!" Dad shouted, his voice fake-cheery. "What say we go for ice cream?"

Mason's gaze stayed locked on Towaco.

Madeline turned to Dad. "I just hate this! Maybe it was a mistake to let Mason get so attached to that horse in the first place. It's too hard on him to say good-bye."

"They're coming back, Madeline," Dad reasoned.

"*He* doesn't understand that, Jack!" she snapped.

I don't like to hear her say "Jack." She's the only one who calls him that. While I was becoming Winnie the Horse Gentler, my dad was changing from the Wyoming Mr. Jack Willis, insurance boss, into Odd-Job Willis, Ashland's handyman. I'd rather hear Madeline call Dad "Odd-Job" than "Jack." Mom called him Jack.

Towaco followed Hawk into the large, padded trailer.

"Don't forget to stop and let him walk around," I pleaded as Hawk walked back down the ramp. We shoved the tailgate shut. "And don't let your dad drive fast."

Hawk grinned at me and pulled from her pocket a small box wrapped in fancy Christmas paper. "Don't open it until Christmas."

"Thanks, Hawk." I wished I'd done my shopping earlier. But at least this year, for the first time in my 12 and a half years, I had my own Christmas money. I'd managed to save from the fees I'd gotten for training horses and boarding Towaco. "You'll get yours as soon as you get back, okay?" I said as I watched Hawk get into the car with her dad.

Dad, Madeline, and I waved as the black trailer bounced away and disappeared around the corner. Only Mason stood stone still, not waving, staring as if he could still see the spots on Towaco's back.

"Want to come with us to get something to eat, Winnie?" Dad asked as Madeline herded Mason toward their van. "We're picking up Lizzy from Geri's house." Lizzy is my "little" sister, a year younger than me, but two inches taller. She also got the great hair and skipped the freckles. Life is so unfair.

"Yes, come with us," Madeline agreed, still pushing Mason toward the van.

I didn't like doing family-like stuff with Madeline. She's tall and too skinny and nowhere near as pretty as Mom was, but she's okay. It's just that I don't think I'll ever get used to Dad having a friend who's a girl.

Note to self: not *a girlfriend.*

"No thanks," I finally answered. "I've got to get to the pet store."

I walked from our house at the edge of town through snow flurries to Pat's Pets in town. Passing by houses with Christmas lights and manger scenes, I saw baby Jesuses everywhere. I did a mental checklist of Christmas gifts I wanted to buy. It helped keep my mind off Hawk and the trailer and the snow.

Ashland doesn't have a lot of stores, and I refuse to buy things from A-Mart, which is owned by the Spidells. They own half of the businesses in town, including Stable-Mart, a fancy stable where horses are held prisoners in their stalls with almost no turnout time. What I needed to do was shop around on the Internet.

Stepping into Pat's Pets felt like changing seasons. Dogs yapped in the back, birds squawked, and the whole store smelled like spring. I hung my damp jacket on the coatrack and shook snow out of my hair. "Pat?"

"Like, hi." Catman Coolidge didn't look up from the computer. He was speed-typing, using only his thumbs and pinkies. Catman and I help man the Pet Help Line, answering e-mails people write in about their pets. He takes the cat questions. I handle the horse questions. And Eddy Barker answers questions about dogs.

"Hey, Catman!" I watched over his shoulder while he answered his last e-mail. I wondered if the people writing him had any idea what he looks like. Catman is a throwback to the 60s or 70s when people used to dress funny and protest war. He has long, wavy, blond hair and eyes as blue as a Siamese cat's. He's probably the only eighth-grader in the world who still wears tie-dyed shirts, striped bell-bottoms, and flip-flops, even in the winter.

Someone had written in:

> Dear Catman,
>   My cat doesn't understand a word I say, and I can't understand her meows. Can you give me a quick course in cat talk?
> —LonelyCat

I watched Catman's fingers fly over the keys as he answered:

> Be cool, LonelyCat!
>   If your cat's meowing, she's talking to

you! Cats meow at humans. They hiss, purr, and growl at other cats. High-pitched sounds mean "Hi." Low-pitched "ow" means "Watch out, man! Don't mess with me." Keep *your* voice high. Cats dig about 50 human words. That's plenty.
—The Catman

Catman logged off. "M wants to know if Hawk and Towaco split." He nodded to the corner of the store, where his buddy sat cross-legged, typing away on a laptop. As usual, M wore black from head to toe.

I hadn't heard M say anything, but I answered him anyway. "Hey, M! They just left."

I think he raised an eyebrow, which is talk-ative for M. As far as I know, nobody has any idea what the *M* stands for. He never says much, except for once in a school debate when he blew us away by speaking like a professor.

I caught a glimpse of a brown curl popping over the counter in the middle of the store. "Pat?"

Pat Haven stood up to her full five-foot height. "Winnie! I didn't see you! Reckon I'm getting blind as a bat! No offense." Pat always

9

excuses herself to the animals in her expressions. "Hawk get off okay?"

I nodded. I'd been trying to put Hawk and Towaco and their snowy trailer ride out of my mind. These questions about her weren't helping. "Mind if I use the computer for a little Christmas shopping?"

"Chill, Horse Gentler," Catman said flatly. "You got mail."

I sighed. "Guess I can shop *after* the horse e-mails." Usually I can't wait to answer the horse questions. I love my job at the pet store. But today I wanted to order Christmas gifts. I only had two and half weeks until Christmas, so I was already cutting it close.

Catman turned the computer over to me, and I logged on. It looked like Barker had already answered the dog mail. I started working my way through the horse questions.

Dear Winnie,
   My horse's feet stink! Is there such a thing as horse-foot deodorant for him?
—PonyGal

Dear PonyGal,
   Stinky hooves are serious. Your horse

might have thrush, an infection that makes the hoof break down and fall apart. Is your horse's stall too wet or dirty? Move him to clean, dry ground. Keep the lines of the frog clean (the grooves that make a V on the bottom of the foot). If the hoof looks black or has runny stuff inside, call your vet!
—Winnie

I had just finished answering the last horse e-mail and was about to run a search on invention magazines for my dad's Christmas gift when the *ding* went off. Another e-mail. I thought about leaving it for next time. Then I imagined a horse in trouble. I clicked on New Mail.

To Winnie the Horse Gentler:
     There's an old horse who looks kinda sick.
     And I know the mean owner won't give a lick.
     So now he's ready to sell it for glue.
     You better write quickly and tell me what to do.
—Topsy-Turvy-Double-U

My first reaction was to jump through the screen and save that horse. Then I read the rhyming note again. Chances were, it was a hoax. Somebody like Summer Spidell and her crowd could have been playing a practical joke. Still, I couldn't risk letting it go unanswered.

Dear Topsy-Turvy,
Do whatever you can to buy that horse. If you can't keep it, give it away to somebody who can.
—Winnie the Horse Gentler

I tried to get my mind back on shopping. The e-mail probably wasn't real, and I really did want to get into the Christmas spirit.

Right away I found the perfect gift for Dad—a one-year subscription to *Gizmo Magazine*. He'd brought back a sample copy from the Invention Convention in Chicago, where he'd met Madeline. Dad had read that magazine so much, pages were scattered all over our house.

I'd already asked Pat to order a special terrarium for Lizzy. I'd never have enough money to get her the iguana too. But the terrarium was the expensive part. And my sister, who loves lizards and all reptiles, would want to pick out her own iguana anyway.

That left Pat. I did a search on cowboy hats and found one store with over 4,000 of them.

"Catman, do you think Pat would like this?" I glanced where M had been sitting. He was gone, and so was Catman.

Shrugging, I bookmarked my favorite hat. Pat would love it in red.

I bounced around the Internet, trying to get ideas for Barker and Catman and Hawk. Nothing seemed right.

"You still at it?" Pat asked. I hadn't heard her walk up.

"Pat, did Lizzy's terrarium come yet?"

She shook her head, sending a stray curl across her forehead. She blew it back up. "That iguana company's slow as snails, no offense."

The store, which had been full of customers when I'd walked in, was almost empty now. "What time is it?"

"Almost two."

"You're kidding!" I started to get up when the mail alert sounded again.

"You can leave that till tomorrow if you want,

Winnie," Pat suggested, heading to the door to meet a customer.

But I couldn't leave the note. I'd wonder all night if I'd left a horse in distress. I clicked on the e-mail and read the subject heading:
EMERGENCY!

I stared at the capital letters until they blurred, until I could force myself to read the message:

> Go home! Now! Run! Run straight to your pasture! NOW!

I stood up so fast the computer chair flipped over. My knees felt weak. An emergency? In my pasture?

Nickers!

$\mathcal{W}$innie?" Pat called.

I dashed out of the pet store. I didn't stop to pull on my gloves. All I could think about was Nickers. What if something had happened to her?

I tried to picture the e-mail message, but my mind hadn't taken a photo of it. Nothing came. I knew it told me to run to the pasture. Had it mentioned my horse?

My feet slid out from under me. I crashed to the sidewalk. Scrambling up, I made my legs keep going.

Snow floated down. White, like Nickers. My eyes stung. My head throbbed, as if my white Arabian were prancing inside my skull.

God, please . . . don't . . . Nickers is so . . .

15

I tried to get a prayer to come out, but the words jumbled. It was like every time I tried to answer a question in English class or give a book report. I couldn't make people understand what I wanted to say. Only this was different. I knew God heard the words before they left my heart.

A horn honked. I slipped again.

"Winnie! Want a ride?"

I glanced to the street, surprised to see cars, people, familiar things.

A van rolled to the curb. Mr. Barker had his elbow out the window. Snow stuck to his close-cropped black hair. "Are you okay?"

"I have to go to Nickers!" I shouted, bolting off the sidewalk, across an empty lot, away from Main Street.

Somebody, Eddy Barker I think, hollered after me, but I couldn't hear him. His words mixed with the snowflakes and drifted away.

I couldn't stop running. My heart shuddered as I turned onto our street. Everything was white. It reminded me of the first time I'd seen my horse, right after we'd moved to Ashland. She was wild then, Wild Thing, running in a white fog. I'd known then that I had to have her.

Nickers was everything to me. If anything had happened to her . . .

I made my way across our lawn, booby-trapped with old tires and car parts under the white snow, works-in-progress for Odd-Job Willis.

I heard a car coming up the street behind me, but I didn't look. I raced for the barn, the closest route to the pasture.

"Nickers!" I screamed.

A crow burst from a bare branch. The flap of its wings echoed like the last sound on earth.

I dashed into the barn, the words pounding my brain: *Run to the pasture!* Once inside, I had to stop. Snow glare had blinded me.

In the stillness I heard a nicker, the most beautiful sound in the whole world.

"Nickers?" *Please let it be Nickers.*

She nickered again. The sound rattled my heart. My hands shook.

Racing to her stall, I spotted her. She was lit from behind by the sun breaking through the connecting paddock. Her mane waved as she tossed her head and sneezed.

I burst into her stall and wrapped my arms around her. "Nickers, Nickers," I cried into her already wet neck. Snowflakes from the pasture had melted into her white winter coat. The smell of wet horse filled my lungs as they heaved with sobs. "Thank you, God. She's all right. Everything's all right."

"Winnie, what's wrong?" Eddy Barker ran into the barn, stopping like I had, his big brown eyes blinking. His Cleveland Indians cap, worn backward, was white with snow.

"Barker, over here!" I called. Only somebody like Eddy Barker—or Catman—would have chased me down to make sure I was okay.

Barker's dad trotted into the barn, bumped into his son, and almost knocked him down. "Is she here?"

Like father, like son. Like mother too. The Barkers are the nicest family I know. The parents teach African-American studies and art and poetry and even computer science at Ashland University. Mr. Barker still looks like the football player he was in college. And Barker is getting more like him every day.

"I'm in the stall with Nickers!" I called. "She's okay. Everything's all right." I swiped my tears with the back of my hand. My fingers were numb and tingly.

"You had us worried," Mr. Barker said in his deep voice.

"Man, Winnie!" Barker came into the stall with Nickers and me. "I thought something awful had happened."

"Me too," I explained. "Somebody played a horrible trick on me." I could almost feel the knot of fear in my stomach turn into a fireball of anger. "I got this urgent e-mail on the help line, telling me to run to the pasture. I can't remember the words exactly, but it made me think something was wrong with Nickers."

Mr. Barker joined us in the stall. He stroked Nickers' jaw. I don't think I'd ever seen him with my horse. It was a nice picture—black against white. I sighed. Nickers was safe.

"I'm sorry somebody put you through that, Winnie," Mr. Barker said softly.

"Why would anybody do that?" Barker asked. "I don't get it."

"Mark's in the car, Winnie," Mr. Barker said. "We should get going. You heard that Irene had puppies while we were in Texas over Thanksgiving? One needs a shot. We're on our way to the vet's."

Irene is Mark's chocolate Lab, and Mark is

one of Barker's five brothers. Barker trained a dog for each of them.

"Thanks for following me home, Mr. Barker," I said.

"I want to take a look around before we go." Barker was already moving through the stall toward the pasture. "Somebody mean enough to get you upset like that could be dumb enough to stick around and see the result." He glanced at his dad. "I'll just take a minute."

"Dad?" Mark Barker shuffled into the barn. He was holding a squirmy, black puppy. Mark's pretty big for a seven-year-old. He walked over to us, smiling Barker's smile.

I had to pet the puppy. It licked my hand. "He's so cute, Mark!"

"His name is Zorro," Mark said proudly.

"Mark, I told you it might be easier on you if you didn't name the puppies," his dad warned.

"I'm keeping all of them," Mark snapped.

Mr. Barker sighed. "We've been all through this, Mark. What on earth would we do with three more dogs? We'll find good homes for them. I promise."

Mark shook his head.

I felt for him. Back in Wyoming, Mom and

I had the same problem. We had tried to keep from naming the horses, too, hoping it would keep us from getting too attached. But it never worked.

"Dad! Winnie!" Barker shouted from the pasture. "Come out here!"

Mr. Barker ducked under Nickers' neck to get to the back of the stall where the open stall door led to the paddock. "Maybe Eddy caught somebody!"

"Stay, Nickers," I whispered, hurrying out to the paddock after Mr. Barker. I didn't want to miss this. If it was Summer Spidell, she was really going to be sorry.

I stopped beside Mr. Barker. We shielded our eyes from the glare and gazed into the pasture.

"Eddy?" Mr. Barker called.

"Over here!" Barker's voice came from the back of the pasture.

I took off running for him. "Barker? Who is it? Don't let 'em go!"

I glimpsed Barker next to somebody . . . or something. As they came into focus, I could see that he was standing next to a horse!

"Look what I found!" Barker shouted. "I didn't know you got another horse, Winnie."

I walked up to the horse, a dapple-gray mare, her head hung low, eyes half shut. Her tangled mane twisted against the thickest winter coat I'd ever seen. The poor thing looked beaten down, even though she stood at about 16 hands. Her backbone stuck up, and her belly sagged down. Even under the fur, ribs showed high on her sides.

Amazed, I stared into her glazed eyes.

"Is it sick?" Barker asked, his hand on the mare's withers. "It doesn't look that good to me."

Mr. Barker walked up. "Another horse? Where did you get it, Winnie?"

"I didn't," I managed to say. "I have no idea where this horse came from."

"You're kidding!" Mr. Barker said.

Barker was pulling at something caught in the mare's mane. "Hey, look at this!" He pulled at a skinny red ribbon. A tiny bow appeared. Below it was an index card with a message scrawled in pencil:

To Winnie the Horse Gentler—Don't look a gift horse in the mouth.

I stared at the crooked letters dangling from the red ribbon. "It doesn't make any sense. Who would give me a horse?"

"Maybe it's an early Christmas gift from your dad?" Barker suggested.

I laughed. "No way. Not *my* dad." Dad didn't like horses much more than Lizzy did. It was Mom who loved horses. Dad already thought I spent too much time with four-legged creatures. He always accuses me of having more horse friends than kid friends, which is true. But it's not a bad thing. Horses have noble character.

"I don't think Winnie's dad would pick *this* horse," Mr. Barker reasoned. "It really doesn't look healthy, does it?"

"Easy, girl," I murmured.

23

The mare jerked away, nose to the sky.

Barker scurried out of the way.

"Careful, Winnie!" Mr. Barker cried.

"I won't hurt you," I cooed. "Poor baby's been hurt by humans. She's headshy, that's all." I scratched her withers, but she didn't seem to notice. She was too intent on keeping her head out of reach, safe from whatever people had done to her.

I tried scratching her back, her shoulder, her rump, and her neck before finding her soft spot on her chest. My mom had taught me that every horse has a secret spot that feels so good when you scratch it they'll forget everything else and be grateful.

As I scratched her chest, the mare slowly lowered her head. Without stopping my scratching, I reached my free hand to scratch her jaw too. She jerked away but lowered her head again. After a minute she allowed me to stroke her forehead.

I traced my finger to the top of her head, over the poll, to a spot just behind her ears. She let me rub her ears and get a good feel of them to tell if she was cold or feverish. She felt okay.

"What's wrong with her, Winnie?" Mr. Barker asked. He glanced back toward the barn, where Mark stood with his puppy.

"I think she's starving, for one thing." I eased past Barker and pointed to her sharp backbone. Part of her rump had bare patches on it, where she'd rubbed the hair off. "She's probably dehydrated too—not enough water." Gently I pinched a fold of skin in front of the flank, then let it go. "See? If the fold flattens out right away, she's got enough water. But it's holding the wrinkle. I have to get her to drink."

I led her toward the barn by her crude, dirty rope halter. She stumbled and heaved. A rasping came from her belly and nostrils. I could tell by the slope of her jaw that she was old. But her legs were surprisingly well muscled, as if she'd been fit once upon a time.

She followed me inside, past Mark. Zorro yapped, but the dapple didn't care.

"Whose is it?" Mark asked.

"I wish I knew, Mark." I put her in Towaco's stall, next to Nickers, who was snorting and pawing the ground.

Nickers squealed at the intruder. But when she stuck her head over the divider to see the enemy, she changed her mind. She nickered like she knew the mare was in trouble.

"You know . . . ," Barker said, as if thinking out loud, "maybe somebody dumped the horse in your pasture because they knew you'd take care of it."

Something clicked inside my brain. "That's it! Barker, the Pet Help Line!"

He frowned at me.

"This morning! I got an e-mail."

He nodded. "You told us. An e-mail that said to run to the pasture—"

"Not that e-mail! Before that one! Somebody wrote me about a horse that was about to go to slaughter. I told them they should give it to somebody who could take care of it! You think this is *that* horse?"

We all turned to the old mare, as if she could give us the answers.

"Makes sense," Barker commented.

"Were both e-mails from the same person?" Mr. Barker asked.

I tried to remember. "I didn't even look at who sent the emergency message. I was so worried about Nickers, I just ran out of the store."

"Who sent the first one?" Barker asked.

I offered the mare water and tried to think. I repeat: Having a photographic memory is *not* the same thing as having a good memory. If my brain doesn't snap a picture—and it hadn't—I'm on my own. "Something like . . . *upside down* . . . no, that's not it. *Topsy-turvy!* It was from Topsy-Turvy something, Barker!"

"I'll check the help line e-mails on our home computer," Barker offered. "At least we can find out if the messages came from the same person."

The mare drank in long gulps. I pulled her head up so she wouldn't choke.

"Let's get going then," Mr. Barker said, herding Mark and Zorro out of the barn. "I'll bet you can track those e-mails as soon as we get back from the vet's, Eddy. Maybe your mother can help."

I heard them drive off. If anybody could use the computer to track down the owner of this "gift horse," it was Barker.

The mare stretched her neck and coughed, gagging at the end of it. I wanted to help, but all I could do was watch and scratch her. She closed her eyes, and her ears lopped to the sides, meaning *I don't feel good, and it doesn't even matter*.

If I ever found out who'd taken such rotten care of her, they'd be sorry.

I fed the gift horse the richest feed we had in the barn. She nuzzled it but didn't take much. I'd only had her for a few minutes and already my heart ached for her. "You're safe now, girl," I murmured.

A cat mewed. Then several cats growled. I knew without turning around that Catman was in the barn.

Note to self: Catman Coolidge could grow up to be a successful cat burglar.

"Look at this, Catman," I said, without turning around.

He moved soundlessly to the stall. "Far out!"

"Can you believe it? Someone just left this poor, sick horse in my pasture—with a bow around her neck!" I turned back to the horse and inched my hand up her chest to her cheek.

She jerked her head up. I waited until her muscles relaxed and her head drooped back down. Then I tried again, moving my fingers slowly until I reached her muzzle. I lifted her lip and checked her gums, which had shrunk, making her teeth look long.

Catman stepped right up and peered into the mare's mouth. "Long in the tooth?"

"The older a horse gets, the more the gums pull up. It makes the teeth look long." I pressed my thumb against the gum above her front teeth, held it a few seconds, and let it go. "Look how the gum stays white. The color should have come right back. Whoever had this horse didn't give her enough water."

I told Catman about the e-mails. "Barker thinks they're from the same person. He's trying to track whoever it is on the Internet."

I slid my fingers to the sides of the mare's mouth. "See the spaces between the teeth and the way her lower incisors are worn almost to the gums? She's old, all right."

"How old?" Catman asked.

I increased pressure on the sides of her mouth until she opened for me. I pointed to the groove on the surface of the upper incisor. "That's the Galvayne's groove. It's the best way to tell a horse's age. The groove doesn't even show up until a horse is 10. Then it works down the tooth a little each year. Halfway down is 15. At 20, the line reaches the bottom. Then the groove starts fading again. At 25, you can only see it in the bottom half of the tooth, and it's gone by age 30."

I let go of her mouth and scratched her chest. "She's about 21."

"Groovy!" Catman exclaimed.

"Not so groovy when you're starved, dehydrated, and who-knows-what else." I didn't want to feel so much for the mare already. At least I hadn't named her yet.

"Winnie, are you out here?" Dad walked into the barn, carrying Mason on his shoulders. "Mason wanted to—" Dad stopped cold.

Mason squirmed off Dad's shoulders and wriggled to the ground. Dad didn't seem to notice. He was staring at the old, gray mare.

If I'd had any doubts whether the horse could possibly have come from my dad, there was no doubt now.

"What's that?" he finally asked.

"Horse," Catman answered.

Dad walked closer, frowning at the horse as if he'd never seen one before. "Where did it come from? Did you get another problem horse?"

"Well, she *is* a problem," I admitted.

Mason ran to the stall. "Towaco?" he asked. But you could tell by the way his shoulders sagged as he peered into the stall that Mason knew the horse wasn't his beloved Towaco. Still he didn't leave. He stared at the mare, his blue eyes huge through his glasses.

"What's going on, Winnie?" Dad's voice had an edge now.

So I told him the whole story, except for the part about how scared I'd been when I thought something had happened to Nickers. "She's really sick, Dad—starved and dehydrated, but maybe worse. I'm just trying to get her to eat and drink."

The whole time I was talking, Mason kept saying, "Horse! Horse!" and getting louder and louder. He stuck his hand under the stall door and tried to pet the mare.

"Mason!" Dad scooped the kid up and held him like a football. "Winnie, I'm going to Loudonville for a while. This horse cannot stay here! Find out who dumped that animal here and give it back."

"We're trying to find—," I started.

"Not good enough." He glanced at Mason, who twisted in his arms, trying to get down.

31

"This is all we need—a sick horse to get attached to." He hoisted Mason higher. "Winnie, if you haven't found the owner by the time I get back, we'll have to call the animal-control people in Mansfield. This isn't our problem."

"That's not fair!" I cried. Everybody knew how the animal-control people *controlled* unwanted animals.

Dad started off, then turned back. "Life's not always fair, Winnie. You have until I get back."

I wanted to run after my dad, but I knew it wouldn't have done any good. He was on a mission—Madeline's mission—to protect and defend Mason, no matter the cost.

Even though it made me as angry as a weaned colt, I understood what Dad was afraid of. He didn't want Mason to get attached to this horse and then have it . . . I couldn't finish, couldn't go there. Life would be a lot better if horses . . . and people . . . never had to die.

I don't remember fighting with Dad in Wyoming. But then I don't remember seeing much of him either. He'd leave for his insurance office before Lizzy and I got up, and sometimes he wouldn't get home until we were in bed.

After Mom died, Lizzy was about the only

thing holding our family together. Dad and I stopped trying.

It wasn't until we'd settled in Ashland that things started getting better between Dad and me. But even now, every time we start "joining up," which is what horse people call it when they bond with their horses, something like this happens.

"Gotta split." Catman set down Nelson, my black barn cat.

"Catman, help Barker find the owner of this horse!" I begged.

He shrugged. Then he left.

After giving the dapple more water, I went in the house and phoned Barker. Matthew, the nine-year-old, answered, and I asked for Barker.

"He's gone," Matthew informed me.

"Where?"

"To see Ralph at the shelter." Ralph Evans is the in-between pastor at our church, but he also runs the local animal shelter.

"Did he track my e-mail from the help line?" I asked, hoping Barker was hot on the trail.

"I'm not my brother's secretary." Matthew is the only Barker who says stuff like that. I could

34

picture his face, scrunched into a frown, kind of like his bulldog's.

"Thank you, Matthew," I said sweetly and hung up. I hustled back to the barn, grabbed the hackamore, and hurried to Nickers. "Let's go see Barker."

"Me too." Catman appeared in the stallway, scaring the life out of me. He walked to the bale of hay at the end of the aisle and stood on it. "Double."

I'd only ridden Nickers double once, a short ride with my dad holding on for dear life. And I was pretty sure the Catman had never ridden double *or* single. But I could use all the help I could get.

Before slipping the bitless bridle on Nickers, I made sure the new mare—it took all my will-power not to name her—had plenty of oats and water. Then I swung up bareback and rode Nickers to the bale of hay. Catman slid on behind me, as silently as he walks.

We rode out of the barn and into the snow. The ground didn't feel icy or slippery, and the only flakes in the air now were blown from trees and roofs—pretend snow. I was glad for Hawk's sake. She and Towaco would be safely out of the snowstorms by now. One less thing to worry about.

Ralph's animal shelter was about a mile out of town, past our house, which is the last house in Ashland. Nickers walked until I was sure Catman wasn't about to fall off. He didn't put his arms around my waist and hold on like Dad had.

"You okay, Catman?" I hollered back.

He leaned back, his palms on Nickers' rump. "Groovy, man!"

I let Nickers trot on the side of the road. Catman still didn't hold on, although I felt him bouncing behind me. "I dig this big time!" he hollered to the sky.

My nose felt numb, but the rest of me soaked up the warmth of Nickers beneath me. We passed a huge manger decoration on the Pentos' front lawn. They're an older couple from our church. Mary and Joseph and the baby looked happy and safe, as if nothing could possibly go wrong in that scene.

It didn't take long to reach the gray building in the middle of nowhere. If somebody missed the Animal Shelter sign out front, they might think this was a storage shack.

I rode up to the hitching post Ralph had put

up for Amish buggies. Catman slid off, and I followed him, looping the reins over the rail. I kissed Nickers and stroked her beautiful Arabian jowls. "Be right back, girl."

I walked in after Catman, and the noise almost sent me back outside. Dogs barked, cats screeched, birds squawked. Something I couldn't identify growled. Something croaked. The overall effect was 10 times louder . . . and smellier . . . than Pat's Pets.

"Ralph!" I yelled, glancing over cages and wondering where Catman had gone.

"We're over here!" Lizzy's voice came from behind the cat cages.

I ducked through rows of creatures until I spotted my sister and her friend Geri with Ralph Evans. He had something in his hand. I moved in closer and saw he was holding a frog, wrapping a white bandage around its long, green frog leg.

Geri glanced up, her eyes misty. "Hamlet broke his leg." Her blonde hair was braided, just like Lizzy's brown hair was. She stood almost as tall as my sister.

Lizzy put her arm around her friend. If they'd been horses, they would have been the

Camargue sisters. Camargues roam wild in the marshes of France. They're surefooted, but high-stepping and beautiful. My sister had probably walked here in the snowstorm, but every hair was in place. I felt my hair, which was about the same color as Lizzy's. But mine had escaped from its rubber band without me noticing. "Hamlet will be fine now, right, Ralph?" Lizzy asked.

Ralph Evans is shorter than my dad but weighs more. At the shelter he wears a white lab coat over blue jeans. His thick, black hair is straight, but it can't make up its mind which way to grow. Ralph's small, brown eyes are set deep, close to his rounded nose. When he's not smiling, which isn't very often, it looks like all his features slide to the middle of his face. It might look weird on somebody else. But one look at Ralph, and you know he'd be a friend for life.

"There you go, Hamlet!" He handed the frog to Geri. "Good as new! He'll be hopping in no time!"

Geri looked relieved, like she believed him. I guess Ralph Evans is a hard man not to believe.

"So what brings you and Catman to our little

home-away-from-home for animals, Winnie?" he asked.

Catman appeared behind Lizzy. He was holding three kittens.

With Lizzy and Geri looking on, I told the whole story again—all about the gift horse, the e-mails, everything I knew. "Matthew told me Barker was on his way over here. I was hoping he was onto something."

"Haven't seen him," Ralph said, stroking Hamlet with his finger.

"Well, I think it's the most beautiful story I've ever heard!" Lizzy declared. "A gift horse! You should call her Gifty! Or Giftus . . . something like that anyway. I hope she gets over being sick though. Nobody should be sick at Christmas." She stroked Hamlet too. The frog huddled in Geri's hands. "Remember Mrs. Purdy in Iowa— or was it Indiana? One of the *I* states we lived in before coming here. Anyway, Mrs. Purdy's cat got so sick—"

The door opened and in came Eddy Barker. "Ralph! I was—hey! You guys are all here, huh?" He came over to us and pulled a computer printout from his pocket.

"Did you find out who gave me the horse,

Barker?" I tried to read upside down as he unfolded the paper.

"Well, those two e-mails came from the same person: *Topsy-Turvy-Double-U.*"

"That's it!" I agreed, remembering now.

"And you never got one from him before—or her. I tried to e-mail back, but I just got an Out of Office reply."

"So we're back to nowhere," I said, disappointed. I turned to Ralph. "Do you have any idea where this horse might have come from?"

Ralph shook his head. "I know folks who mistreat horses, but I wouldn't send you there. I've called the humane society on them a couple of times. Not much else I can do. We're not set up for big animals here."

I knew that. Mansfield Animal Control took the big animals and "controlled" them.

"I need to get Hamlet home," Geri said. "Sorry. Hope your horse gets better."

Lizzy started to follow her. Then she turned back. "Ralph, tell them about the Christmas Eve service!"

Ralph grinned. "It's going to be a good one. Special music by Miss Elizabeth Willis!"

"Cool, Lizzy!" Catman called after her, as she

and Geri put on their coats and hats. He turned to Ralph. "What's a Christmas Eve service?"

Other pastors might have said something like, "Haven't you ever been to one?" But not Ralph. He didn't miss a beat, but just explained. "Well, Barker's going to read the Scripture about Jesus being born. And we have music, like Lizzy singing 'Amazing Grace'."

Lizzy, one hand on the doorknob, shouted, "That's it! You can call that new horse Grace! Amazing Grace!" Then she and Geri left.

I didn't want to give the mare a name, but I had a feeling this one was going to stick, like it or not.

"What else do you do?" Catman asked.

"We worship, eat, sing, pray, eat some more," Ralph explained.

"Far out!" Catman declared, carrying the kittens back to their mom.

I wasn't sure what to do next. Time was running out. Dad would be back, and I still wasn't any closer to finding out who'd left the horse. "Barker, isn't there anything else you can try?"

"I'll hit a couple of reverse directories. You know, key in the e-mailer's name and see if I get a hit on Ohio users. I'll let you know if I come up with something."

At least I could tell Dad that. I hoped it would be enough.

Barker stayed at the shelter to help Ralph with a dog somebody had dropped off. Catman and I rode Nickers home in silence, the only sound, the padded *crunch* of her hooves on snow. Somebody should record that sound and make a million dollars.

When we got close to my house, I was relieved to see that Dad's truck wasn't back yet. When Dad sold the ranch in Wyoming, we left almost everything, including our car, there. We'd driven the cattle truck all the way to Ohio, zigzagging through shorter stays in the *I* states— Illinois, Indiana, and Iowa.

Catman and I rode into the barn and slid off Nickers. I brushed her and turned her loose in the pasture. She ran off, her neck arched, tail flagged high, prancing and snorting. I could have watched her all day.

But that mare needed me.

Catman, seven or eight cats milling around at his feet, was already in the stall with the dapple-gray mare. "Check it out, man!" He pointed to the mare's sagging belly. "You sure this dude's grub deprived?"

"I was thinking she might have heaves. That would explain the belly and the cough." I hadn't had time to really examine the mare. I moved my hand up her chest to her neck and down her back. "Her spine's sharp. She's starving, all right."

The mare watched me, her eyes like pond water after I've thrown in a rock. Wrinkles circled her eyelids like pond ripples.

I checked her hooves, which needed work. They flared, as if she'd foundered from neglect more than once, softening the hoof.

Catman was right. Gracie—the mare—sure did have a swollen belly. I touched it, and her ears shot back, saying, *Cut it out!*

"Sorry," I told her, checking her rump and haunches, the stifle and cannon. "You're going to be just fine."

One ear flopped forward, saying, *Promise?*

She let me run my hand down her back leg. I squatted and peered underneath her. "Wait a minute. . . ." I blinked, then looked again. Her udders were tight, swollen. "Talk to me, girl."

"What's the skinny?" Catman asked, squatting on the other side of the mare.

"Winnie! Didn't you hear me calling you?" Dad stormed into the barn.

I knew Dad was waiting for an answer, but I couldn't speak. I couldn't move. I was remembering the way Gracie had walked in from the pasture. Her stride had been a bit too wide.

"Winnie!" Dad's voice sounded foggy, the words coming from far away. "You can't pretend I'm not here. I'm sorry. I really am. I wish you could have tracked down the owner and given him back his own problem."

Veins stood out on Gracie's hairless abdomen. I should have seen it before. "How could I have missed it?" I muttered.

Nickers came into her own stall and poked her head over the divider. She stared, cow-eyed. She'd known all along.

I stood up and moved behind the mare.

"Winnie, what—?" Dad started.

Just then Lizzy and Geri thundered into the barn. "We wanted to see the new horse!" Geri shouted, laughing.

I lifted the mare's tail and let it down again.

"There she is!" Lizzy walked closer but stopped a few feet away. "Hi, Gracie!"

"Gracie?" Dad repeated. "You named her?"

He strode to the stall. "What if I'd brought Mason back? Did you think about that? That poor kid's already sick about losing Towaco. And now he can't stop talking about *this* horse! Winnie! Turn around and look at me!"

I did.

"You can name the horse anything you want," Dad said. "It doesn't change a thing."

"Well, then we need another name. Does *that* change anything?" I asked, all the clues finally coming together in my head.

"Another name?" Dad stared at me like *I'd* just shown up in *his* pasture with a bow around *my* neck. "What are you talking about, Winnie? Why would you need another name?"

"For another horse. There are two of them in this stall."

Even Catman looked at me like I'd lost it.

So I told them. "This mare is about to have a baby."

45

Chapter 5

*F*ar out!" Catman cried from Gracie's stall.

My dad stared at me, speechless.

"A baby!" Lizzy squealed. "That is so amazing! Amazing Grace!"

"I don't think I ever saw a pregnant horse before," Geri commented.

"She can't be!" Dad ran his fingers through his hair. His stocking cap fell off. He didn't pick it up. "You said she was old. She *looks* too old. Maybe you're wrong. Could you be wrong, Winnie?"

I started to say no. Then I thought how that sounded. I shrugged. I'd seen a lot of horses in foal back in Wyoming. And I'd read every horse book that came into the library. I was as sure as I could be.

"So how long does it take?" Geri asked. "I mean, how long are horses pregnant?"

I was grateful for Geri's questions, things that had answers—not like the questions I knew Dad was about to hurl at me. "Usually about 11 months, 340 to 350 days. But once we had a Tennessee Walker who foaled after 10 months and a Quarter Horse who went just over a year."

"Wait now." Dad paced the stallway. "How can we know if you're right about this, Winnie?"

"We can get the vet," I answered. "She needs the vet to check her out anyway."

"That costs money," he said, as if talking to himself.

Money was always tight around our house. Usually Lizzy got to keep her babysitting money, and I kept my money from working the Pet Help Line. But Dad had been fretting about bills all month. People didn't seem to need as many odd jobs done in the winter as in summer, and Dad's inventions hadn't exactly been making the cover of *Gizmo Magazine*. I knew Lizzy used her own money to buy her Christmas-cookie-baking groceries.

"I have money for it, Dad." It was true. I had my Christmas-shopping money. No reason I couldn't scale back a bit on gifts if I had to. Gracie needed a vet. "Hawk paid through December, even though Towaco won't be using up feed or anything."

Dad walked up to Gracie and reached out his hand to pet her. The horse jerked back so fast, she plowed into me.

Dad stepped back and shook his head. "Call the vet."

I called the vet, but Doc Stutzman was out on a call—to Spidells' Stable-Mart. When I phoned Spidells', all I got was the answering machine.

In the kitchen Lizzy and Geri were already starting a new batch of cookies. Whatever kind they were baking smelled great.

"Did you get the vet?" Lizzy hollered over.

"No. I'm going to ride over to Stable-Mart and talk to him."

I hurried back to the stall and bridled Nickers. Catman, without saying a word, went to his hay bale at the end of the stallway. Nickers eased by the bale, and Catman jumped on behind me. We trotted the whole way to Spidells'.

Something icy passes through me every time I glimpse the huge, sterile stables where Spidells raise and board expensive "assets" and never let horses be horses. When we first moved to Ashland, I got a job mucking stalls there. It killed me to watch horses go bonkers because they only got outside a few minutes a day.

Summer Spidell, in a leather coat, her long, blonde hair tucked under a matching leather cap, leaped out from the stables as we rode up. Her face was as tan as it was in summer. She was the only person in Ashland who actually went into the Tan-Fast-ic tanning salon. "What do you think you're doing here?"

"Nice to see you too, Summer," I offered. "Is Doc Stutzman around?"

She glared at me as if she hadn't heard my question. "I've been looking high and low for you, Winifred Willis!"

Note to self: Always avoid the highs and the lows.

"Well," I said, swinging my leg over Nickers' neck and dropping to the ground, "many people are looking for me."

It wasn't true. Many people probably do look for Summer Spidell. She's part of the popular "herd" at school. They band together like Mustangs in the wild, fiercely guarding their precious brood from outsiders . . . like me.

Just then Catman seemed to realize he was

riding solo on a horse that used to be called Wild Thing. He jumped off . . . the wrong side. "That was a blast, Nickers," he whispered.

A shrill whinny pierced the cold air. It came from inside the stables. My first reaction was to run inside.

But Summer blocked my way. "It's just Spidell's Sophisticated Scarlet Lady. The vet is giving the horses their vaccinations."

I felt sorry for Summer's horse, a beautiful but high-strung American Saddle Horse. She squealed again.

"I want to know how many rolls of wrapping paper you've sold, Winifred." Summer's voice sounded pouty.

I'd forgotten about the stupid Christmas-wrapping-paper sale our middle school was doing. It was all Summer's big idea. She'd been lobbying for our classes to do something at the end of the year besides the usual tour of the recycling center. When she came up with the idea that we all go to Cedar Point Amusement Park, Ms. Brumby, our English teacher, ran it by the school administration for their okay and then said we'd have to raise the money.

"I haven't picked up my rolls yet," I admitted. Each roll of fancy wrapping paper cost about four times as much as you can get it for at A-Mart. And since A-Mart is also owned by the Spidells . . . their paper was so expensive, we just wrapped our gifts in the Sunday comics.

Summer sighed, as if she just didn't know what to do with me. "Talk to her, Catman!"

I grinned. She sure didn't know the Catman. He was bound to find the whole sale thing as stupid as I did. "Yeah, talk to me, Catman," I said, trying to imitate Summer's whine. "Tell me this middle-school project is as dumb as I think it is."

Summer looked shocked. "Catman already sold all of his rolls, didn't you, Catman?" She smiled at him, her teeth so white I could have used them for a flashlight.

I glared at Catman, the traitor, then handed him Nickers' reins. "I'm going to see the vet."

"You can't go in there!" Summer called after me.

I kept going.

Summer's horse was in the indoor arena, the only part of Stable-Mart I'd like to own. Richard Spidell, her 16-year-old brother, was shouting at the horse as he jerked a rope attached to a chain-nosed halter. "Get over here, you—!"

Doc Stutzman stood a few feet away, loading two syringes. He was short and stocky, hatless, and already half bald. He'd only been a vet about a year.

Scar, my nickname for Spidell's Sophisticated Scarlet Lady, was putting up a great fight, backing away as Richard jerked the leadrope. Then she reared, stepping toward him on her hind legs.

"Let me try," I urged, coming up behind Richard. The mare's eyes were white with fear and anger.

"Get out of the way, Winnie!" Richard shouted. "You'll get hurt."

He knew better. When I worked at Stable-Mart, I'd calmed horses he couldn't get near. He just didn't want to look bad in front of the new vet.

"Easy, Scar," I said softly.

Her forelegs slammed the sawdust and sprang up again. I had to get Richard out of the way. Scar was too upset with him to give me a chance. So I left Richard to struggle with Scar while I went to work on the vet.

"Winnie, right?" Doc smiled without showing teeth. "How's that Appy at your place?"

Hawk's parents had hired Doc to examine Towaco when the Appy was at my barn.

"Towaco's fine. He and Hawk are showing in Florida next week." I glanced over at Scar, who was in a tug-of-war with Richard. "Doc, can you get Richard to give me a try with that horse?"

A wave of fear crossed Doc's face. I figured he, like everyone else in town, didn't want to risk a falling-out with the richest stable in the county.

"Please?" I begged.

"Well, we're not getting anywhere now," he admitted. He inhaled, then stepped past me. "Richard! I have an idea. Why don't you let the girl try to hold the horse. That mare is probably used to females, since she's Summer's horse."

It was the perfect out for Richard. I wouldn't have thought of it in a hundred years.

"Well, okay," Richard said, pretending not to be relieved. "But I'll be right here if you need me."

"That's a comfort," I muttered as I took the leadrope from him.

Scar jerked back. I kept slack in the rope so she didn't think it was a tug-of-war, like she'd been winning with Richard. Pretty soon she got tired of backing up and stopped.

"Good girl." I edged closer, careful not to look her straight in the eyes.

She snorted.

I moved to her muzzle and blew gently into her nostrils. She tossed her head. She didn't blow back, like Nickers would have or most other horses. But it seemed to calm her. I'd learned the old Native American trick of greeting a horse the way they greet each other from my mom.

"Doc?" I called. "Slip behind me. I think I can keep her calm."

It wasn't like I thought I was Super Horsewoman. It's just that sometimes I can tell what a horse is thinking—more times than I can tell what humans are thinking, anyway. Scar knew I expected her to be good for me. Richard had expected her to act up. Horses live up to what you expect of them.

Doc snuck up behind me. I motioned him to a spot behind my elbow, where Scar wouldn't see the needle. He moved slowly. Still Scar's ears flew flat back, demanding, *What's going on here?*

"You're fine," I assured her. "Just let me do this, and I'll get you away from here." Then I whispered to Doc, "When I lift my arm and act like I'm giving her the shot, you sneak in and do it."

I pretended to give the shot. Doc stuck her. Scar jerked, but she didn't pull away.

"Good girl," I cooed, nodding to Doc to give her the second shot.

"Got it!" Doc announced, stepping away, hiding the syringes behind his back. "I might have to bring you with me for the follow-up booster, Winnie."

"Good, Scar," I said, reaching to scratch her neck.

Like a striking snake, the mare stuck out her head and tried to bite me. I dodged just in time.

"Those shots better not swell this time!" Summer shouted from her safe position on the other side of the arena. "We have a show right after Christmas!"

Doc whispered so only I could hear, "She didn't tell me her horse swelled up from vaccinations. I could have given the shots on opposite sides of the neck, or even on the rump."

I grinned at him, imagining the scene.

He must have been imagining the same thing. "On the other hand, I'll live to give another shot."

There was hope for this vet yet.

I led Scar back to her stall. Nobody objected, not even Scar. But when I let her go, her ears shot back, and she tried to bite me again. *Like owner, like horse.*

When I came back to the arena, Richard was talking to Dr. Stutzman.

As soon as Richard stopped for a breath, I jumped in. "Dr. Stutzman, I need you to come by my place."

"New problem horse?" he asked.

"I've got a horse I'm pretty sure is close to foaling. But she's not in good shape."

He packed up his doctor's bag. "I'll be right over and—"

"You're not finished here," Richard interrupted.

59

Doc snapped his bag shut. "I thought that was the last of them, Richard."

"Two more in the hot walkers," Richard said, picking up Doc's bag and walking out to where Spidells kept their "exerciser." That hot walker looks like a big wagon wheel turned on its side, with the rim kicked off. Horses tied into it plod around in little circles. That way nobody has to ride them. When I worked at Stable-Mart, I made it my mission to free as many horses as I could from that contraption. I didn't work there long.

Summer, still on the other side of the arena, shouted, "You should stay and make sure those shots don't cause ugly lumps."

Doc scratched his head. "Sorry, Winnie. I guess it will be a while before I get to your barn, but I'll get there."

It was as good as I was going to get. "Thanks, Doc."

Outside, Nickers had pulled Catman almost into the stable. I cupped my hands and gave him a leg up. Then I climbed on in front. The temperature must have dropped 10 degrees.

"Can we stop by my pad?" Catman asked.

I knew Richard would keep the vet as long as

he could, so there wasn't any rush. I headed Nickers toward the Coolidges'.

We took the back roads through pastures, across a creek, and up the hill to Coolidge Lane. When Coolidge Castle came into view, Nickers snorted. She'd seen the place before, but even I'm never quite ready for the old house. The first time I saw it, I was sure it was deserted and maybe haunted. All three of its stories need a coat of paint, and a few of the windows are boarded up.

Nickers pawed the ground and pranced in place as we got closer.

"What's wrong, girl?" I asked.

Then I saw what had her spooked. It wasn't the house; it was the Christmas decorations. On the strip of lawn where Mr. and Mrs. Coolidge proudly display lawn ornaments for every season, were more Santas than I'd ever seen. More than existed in the whole town of Ashland. More than the whole state of Ohio, maybe.

"Your folks have outdone themselves," I told Catman.

Not all of the Santas were your typical North Pole variety. I recognized the Seven Dwarfs I'd seen carrying shovels and tools for Labor Day. They sported Santa suits now. There were Santa mice, squirrels, porcupines, foxes, wolves, and a moose. And in the middle stood a Santa bear the size of Rhode Island.

"They've only just begun," Catman warned, sliding off Nickers' rump before I could tell him not to.

"Calvin!" Mrs. Coolidge's voice drifted around the house from the backyard. "We're back here!"

I slid off Nickers, and Catman pulled out some hay he stores under his porch just for Nickers' visits. We left my horse happily munching alfalfa as I followed Catman to the back of the house. There we found Mr. and Mrs. Coolidge, dressed from head to toe in matching red snowsuits. They were patting snow onto the tiniest snowman I'd ever seen, about the size of a colt's head. With only a dusting of snow on the ground, it was amazing they'd been able to pull together enough snow for even that.

"Winnie!" Mrs. Coolidge ran at me, flinging her mittens off as she crossed the back lawn.

I was glad I had my stocking cap on. Claire Coolidge works at a beauty parlor in Ashland, where they still use curlers and make you sit under a hair dryer. For some reason she loves my wild, bushy hair.

"What I wouldn't give for just *this* much hair!" she exclaimed, fingering the ends of my hair that stuck out of my cap. "One of these days when your back is turned, Winnie, I'm going to cut it all off and glue it onto my head!"

Note to self: Never turn your back on Claire Coolidge.

Bart Coolidge, owner of Smart Bart's Used Cars, walked toward us, a camera blocking his face. "Say 'Chevy'!" he commanded. He looked different with his bald head covered by the red hood. But I could see the top of his Tweety Bird tie peeking out of his snowsuit.

"I take a lousy picture," I warned. "What's with the mini-snowman?"

Mrs. Coolidge gasped and dashed back to the snow figure as if it were a child she'd forgotten about. "Contest," she explained.

Catman says his parents earn more from winning contests than from his dad's car business.

Mr. Coolidge knelt in front of the snowman, turned the camera in all directions and snapped, like a modeling session, only the model didn't move. "Vacation for four in lovely Aspen—all expenses paid! First prize for the best snowman. Deadline tomorrow. Not to worry . . . magnifying zoom lens."

He stood up suddenly. "Sa-a-ay! What did Smart Bart say to Santa as the famous used-car salesman, in his '64 Mustang, passed the jolly man and his reindeer on Christmas Eve?"

I was already cracking up. "I give."

" 'You *slay* me!' Get it? You *sleigh* me?" Mr. Coolidge's laugh came in windy puffs, like a horselaugh.

"Time to split," Catman announced.

I tried to follow Catman, but Mr. Coolidge wouldn't let me.

"So," Mr. Coolidge bellowed, like he was playing to a comedy club, "Santa Claus moved to the rain forest and traded in his sleigh for a Chevy convertible from Smart Bart's Used Cars. 'It will be just the thing,' Santa explained, 'for delivering presents all over the world on Christmas Eve!' Mrs. Claus shook her head, obviously not convinced. 'Only if it doesn't *rain, dear.*' " Mr. Coolidge laughed so hard he choked, and his wife had to whack him on the back. "Get it? *'Reindeer'?* I got a million of 'em!"

Once inside Coolidge Castle, a dozen cats swarmed past Catman as he made his way toward the phone. I looked again at the closed red velvet drapes, the huge chandeliers that shone light on the wood floors, the winding staircases, and the old-fashioned furniture that always makes me feel like I've stepped inside a 100-year-old book. Then I ducked down the hall, past tapestry-covered walls, to visit the newest litter of kittens.

I recognized three of the four kittens who came to greet me—Hanson, Griffin, and Miffin. Believe it or not, they're named after the first presidents of the United States. Catman taught me that. Under the *Articles of Confederation*, eight men were elected president for a one-year term each. John Hanson was "the first President of the United States in Congress Assembled."

Catman finished his phone call. Then we took off. I let Nickers trot and even canter back to the barn. I didn't want to miss the vet, just in case he got away from Spidells' sooner than expected.

But when we got there, nobody was in the barn except the poor mare. While I cooled off

Nickers, Catman jumped into the stall with Gracie and brushed her.

When I finished with Nickers, I joined Catman in Gracie's stall and examined her for myself again. "I think she's really close, Catman." When horses are about three weeks away from dropping foal, the udders swell with milk, then go down again. Hers were staying swollen.

When the vet finally showed, he went to the house first, and Lizzy and Dad walked him out to the barn. Doc looked the mare over, took her temperature, and drew blood.

"I'll take this back and run it through the lab," Doc said, holding up the tube of dark red blood. "I could do an ultrasound, but we don't need it. "I think it's safe to say Winnie's right. She's with foal."

"Sweet!" Lizzy exclaimed. "A baby horse! Not that I'll want to cuddle it. I know it's silly, but they still scare me, even the little ones. Still, this is just so . . . so . . . Christmasy!"

"Well, don't get too hopeful," Doc said, stroking the mare's neck. His face looked pained, like he'd seen too much already.

It's what people say about me sometimes. "I can see the pain in your face, Winnie," Pat

Haven had said only a week after we'd moved to Ashland.

"I knew it," Dad muttered. "That horse isn't going to make it, is she, Doctor?"

I glanced at Catman. Then we both turned to Doc Stutzman. I could feel my heart pounding like horses' hooves against my chest. "Tell Dad he's wrong," I whispered.

Doc pressed his lips together, turning them white. "I'm sorry, Winnie. This poor mare is used up. I don't think she can deliver the foal alive. I'm afraid you're going to lose both of them."

*Y*ou're wrong!" I screamed. "She's not *that* sick! And the foal—"

"The foal may be fine now," Doc admitted. "But that doesn't help us much if the mare's too weak to give birth. And she *is* too weak. I think you know that, Winnie."

I wanted to hit him, to make him stop.

"Is there anything you can do?" Dad asked.

Doc shook his head. "I could try a C-section, but the mare would never survive cutting the foal out. And even if we were willing to sacrifice the mare for the foal, I don't think it would work. As malnourished as this mare is, her foal needs every possible day in the womb if it's going to survive outside of the womb."

"Man. Bummer. Downer." Catman paced the stall like a nervous Thoroughbred.

Doc rubbed the mare behind the ears. "They've got a facility at Ohio State that does some experimental procedures. But it's a lot for a mare to go through." He glanced at Dad. "And your bill would be in the thousands. I'm willing to do whatever you decide, hear? I don't like losing an animal any more than you do."

I wanted them all to leave. Even Catman. I couldn't stand seeing the pain in *his* face.

The vet told us to talk about it and let him know if we needed him to "take care of it."

It wasn't until I'd gone to bed and Lizzy was making her weird snoring sounds that Dad tried to talk to me. He must have heard me thrashing around in bed because he tapped on the door and called, "Winnie?"

I pretended to be asleep, but he didn't buy it. He sat on the foot of my bed and said what he'd come to say. "Winnie, I think the best thing is to let the vet take care of this. He'll know the best way to handle the situation so—"

I sat up so fast the bed shook. *"Handle* it? The way animal control would *handle* it? Gracie's not an *it!* And neither is her foal! You can't—!"

"And I won't," Dad said so calmly I wanted to throw my pillow at him. "I won't *make* you call in the vet. But I *will* make you face reality. That horse is almost guaranteed to die, no matter what we do."

"No!" My chest hurt, as if I'd been kicked in the windpipe.

Dad went on like he hadn't heard me. "And the longer you hang on to it—*her*—the more pain you're going to cause yourself and others. We don't need more pain and grief, Winnie—not you, not Mason, not any of us. Not this Christmas."

Tears choked me. I coughed out words like shotgun pellets. "I . . . *you* . . . don't understand. You don't care! I wish . . . I wish Mom were here. *She'd* know. She'd be on my side."

Dad's eyes misted over. Then he got up and walked out of the room.

I threw myself down on my pillow, sobbing, gasping between sobs. At least he wasn't going to make me do it. At least that.

Sunday morning Lizzy made raspberry pancakes in the shape of Christmas wreaths. I tried to swallow a few bites, but I was too anxious to get out to the barn.

"Too bad I'm so scared of horses," Lizzy admitted, pouring homemade syrup on a stack of pancakes. "I could help you more with Gracie. I don't know why horses give me the willies. Anyway, I guess I wouldn't have that much time to help. I'm so busy making Christmas gifts." She set down the bottle of purple syrup. "Are you done Christmas shopping, Winnie?"

I shook my head. I hadn't done a thing about shopping since I'd found the mare in my pasture.

Gracie and Nickers were waiting for me in the barn. I hung out with them until I heard the Barker Bus.

When we moved to Ashland, Lizzy started babysitting for Eddy Barker's little brothers right away. She'd been the first one to go to church with them. After a while, I started going too. Now that Dad was going regularly, we could have driven ourselves. But the Barkers still swung by every Sunday in their giant yellow van we dubbed the Barker Bus.

Lizzy, Dad, and I squeezed into the middle seat with Matthew and Mark. Mr. Barker sat in the back with the littlest Barkers—Luke, Johnny, and William.

We greeted each other. Then I turned to Mark. "How are Irene's puppies doing?"

The van went silent. You'd have thought I'd asked when the world was scheduled to end.

"My puppies are just fine," Mark answered.

"Mark," Mrs. Barker said, tightening her grip on the steering wheel, "we've been over and over this. You're helping Irene take care of *her* puppies until they're old enough to give away to wonderful homes who don't already have five dogs. Right?"

Matthew, the only Barker who doesn't smile a lot, actually chuckled.

"Guess who came over to play with the puppies," Barker shouted from the front. "M!"

"He seems like a nice young man," Mrs. Barker added.

Nobody spoke until Granny B turned from the front seat and said, "Winnie, you're looking troubled, girl."

I nodded. Something about Granny B always makes me feel like she's been discussing me one-on-one with God and he's been telling her things nobody else knows. Even her white hair, sticking out like fresh cotton, looked like the breath of God had just blown right on her.

"I should have called you, Winnie!" Barker shouted over Johnny's demand to be freed from the car seat. "But I'm no closer to finding out who left that horse than I was yesterday."

"You mean *horses!*" Lizzy exclaimed. Then, faster than a horse's trot, she explained all about Gracie and the foal, while Dad stared ahead, stone-faced and tight-lipped.

"Imagine that!" Mrs. Barker, who was driving, peeked at me in the rearview mirror. It framed her face like a movie-star picture. She's really pretty, with deep brown skin, wavy hair, and huge brown eyes.

Mr. Barker leaned forward from the backseat. "I thought that horse looked too old."

"She *is* too old!" Dad snapped, so solemnlike the whole car, except for William, went silent again until we reached the church.

Once inside, we headed for the Barker pew. Halfway down the aisle, I stopped. Catman, who always arrives late and makes a grand entrance to the organ music, was already there. And next to him sat M, in a black turtleneck and black jeans.

As far as I knew, M had never seen the inside of a church. I'd only met his parents once, and I liked them a lot. They made it into the *Mansfield News Journal* and even the *Akron Beacon Journal* from time to time for demonstrating against a nuclear power plant or for boycotting a store that sells the wrong kind of tuna. But they weren't churchgoers.

M scooted about six inches from Catman, and I squeezed between them. I had to sit with my shoulders scrunched to my ears, which may be why I didn't hear all the announcements. Or it might have been because I couldn't get my mind off Gracie.

"Clue us in," Catman whispered. "M wants the skinny on that horse."

I was sitting three millimeters from M and hadn't heard him ask anything, but I relayed what the vet had said.

M shut his eyes.

Ralph Evans greeted us pretty much the same way he welcomes customers to the animal shelter. I like that he doesn't have a Sunday Ralph different from the regular Ralph. He wore a gray shirt instead of the white lab coat. But he talked exactly the same. "I sure hope everybody's coming to the Christmas Eve celebration."

"Right-on!" Catman shouted.

Nobody else shouted anything. But they didn't seem to mind the Catman.

I caught Dad scoping out the back pews and knew he was hoping Madeline and Mason would show up. He'd been inviting them every Sunday, but so far they hadn't made it.

We stood to sing a couple of Christmas carols, which was a relief from being squished in the pew. Then Ralph started his sermon. He'd been giving Christmasy sermons since Thanksgiving.

"Last week we talked about that angel who came to see Mary and give her the big news that she was picked out of everybody to be the mother of God's Son. But I want to tell you about another message Mary got, this one from an old prophet named Simeon. He'd been waiting for the Messiah his whole life. So when Mary and Joseph walked into the temple with their baby, Simeon knew who it was. He told Mary that Jesus would do great things and save all the people. Then he added, like a P.S.: 'And a sword will pierce your very soul.'

"Mary got promised joy and pain, side by side. And you know—we get the same promise. It's part of the same package: life and death; pain of childbirth and the joy of a child born."

That's where I stopped listening and started wondering. Would it be like that with Gracie and her foal? Pain, then joy? Joy, then pain? I didn't want her to suffer. I couldn't stand it if she suffered.

Why couldn't everybody just skip all the pain part and go straight to the joy?

After church, I told Catman and M good-bye, but M followed me to the Barker Bus.

"Need a ride, M?" Mrs. Barker asked. "Hop in."

The whole way to our house M kept up a whispering conversation with Granny B in the front seat. When we got to our house, he hopped out with Dad, Lizzy, and me, although he lives in the government housing apartments on the other side of town.

"You're welcome, M," Granny B called, although I hadn't heard M say thanks.

Dad and Lizzy walked to the house, but I headed straight for the barn. I was wearing a denim dress Lizzy got at Goodwill, so I didn't feel like I had to change.

M followed me.

Nickers whinnied from the pasture and trotted into her stall to meet me. I slipped in with her and hugged her neck, grateful for her fresh, horse smell.

M got into the stall with Gracie.

"She needs exercise, M," I suggested, thinking about the way Mom used to keep the broodmares active right up to foaling.

I handed him a brush and leadrope. He brushed her mane, then looked like he didn't know what to do next.

"You can give her a once-over with the brush. Then lead her outside to the paddock and just walk her around." It occurred to me that I seemed to be answering questions he hadn't asked. Or had he?

The only sounds in the barn were the *swish, swish* of the brushes as we stroked the horses. Nelson, my barn cat, leaped out of nowhere and jumped onto Nickers' back. Catman had given me the little black kitten with one white paw soon after I'd taken over the barn. Catman still has the parent cats, Wilhemina and Churchill. He named my cat Nelson because the real Winston Churchill had a cat named Nelson.

Nickers didn't complain as the cat curled up on her and purred.

"What—? Whoa now!" M, hands up, jumped back from Gracie.

I hurried into their stall. "What's wrong, M?"

He stared at the old mare. His eyes were rimmed with white. If he'd been a horse, he would have been a scared Arabian. "It . . . that is, *she* . . ." He pointed to Gracie's belly.

"Did you feel a kick?" I felt the mare's flank, and M laid his hand next to mine. We didn't move for a long time. Then I felt it. "It kicked!" I cried, biting my lip so I wouldn't bawl like a baby.

M put his head against Gracie's side and listened. "I hear it!" he whispered, grinning. He had dimples. Who knew?

"Everything okay out here?" Lizzy called, trotting into the barn.

"We felt the foal kick, Lizzy!" I said.

"Sweet!" she exclaimed, tiptoeing closer to Gracie's stall and peeking in. "That's good, right?"

"That's great!" I agreed.

M and I listened to Gracie's belly again but didn't hear anything.

"Oh!" Lizzy exclaimed. "I almost forgot why I came out here. Thought you might be hungry." Lizzy does all of our creative cooking.

"What did you make this time, Lizzy?" I asked, my stomach growling.

"Nothing! Madeline and Mason came over and brought pizza. It's just plain pepperoni. But I'll put extra things on for anybody who wants them . . . cherry tomatoes, celery, leftover tuna casserole, potato chips."

M led the way, and Lizzy and I followed him into the house for pizza.

Pepperoni-pizza slices were served on individual, waterproof, battery-operated plates. These "power plates" were Madeline's invention. She won first prize at the Chicago Invention Convention, either for helium furniture or her automatic, house-greeting security system. I can't remember, and I'm not about to ask.

Mason, who hadn't even met M before, sat on his lap and watched him eat pizza slices backwards, starting at the wide, crust end and finishing at the tip. Halfway through my second slice, I heard Mason giggle. He and M had each eaten their slices into the shape of an *M*.

When we finished, Madeline showed us how

the dishes were self-cleaning. Each plate had its own windshield wipers, stuck like rubber hoses to the sides of the plate. She still needed our water though.

Mason followed M when we got up to go back to the barn.

"Come on back, Mason," his mom called.

"Towaco?" Mason asked. Then louder, "Go, Towaco!"

Dad shot me a dirty look, like it was my fault Mason had fallen in love with Hawk's Appaloosa. He and Madeline had been happy enough when horse therapy worked and Mason really got into the riding lessons. Now they both acted like they wished it had never happened.

I knelt down to Mason-level. "Mason, you remember that Towaco's on vacation with Hawk, right? They'll both be back New Year's. Then you can hang out with the Appy again, deal?"

"I want to see the *other* Towaco, the mommy horse," he said softly.

I didn't know what to say. He's so much smarter than we give him credit for. Just from listening to all of us, he must have figured out that Gracie was having a foal. It made me wonder what else he'd figured out.

I'd asked Madeline and Dad about Mason a couple of times, why he was the way he was. Madeline never said much, only that something happened to his head, some trauma, when he was little and that whatever happened to him makes him act autistic sometimes. He can tune out the whole world when he wants to, which I kind of admire.

"Winnie, how could you tell him that horse is having a baby? You know it doesn't have a chance of—" Dad stopped. I imagined smoke coming out of his ears.

"Me? I didn't tell him anything!"

Madeline had one long arm wrapped across her skinny stomach and the other hand over her mouth. "Oh, Mason—"

M reached down, and in one motion, scooped Mason up and onto his shoulders. "Little M," Big M said, "Gracie isn't a mom yet, and she may not be. She's sick. Understand?"

Mason held onto M's black ponytail and nodded. "I understand."

M turned to Madeline. "Barn okay?"

You could tell how much Madeline didn't want to say okay. I think if she had her wish, she'd never let Mason out of the safety of his room, where even the furniture, all helium, can be floated up to the ceiling and out of the way. "Well, I guess," she finally answered. "But be careful!"

Be careful? Brother. There went our master plan of feeding him to the lions.

In the barn, I showed M and Mason where I store the grass hay. The Amish grow it and mow it, leaving in the wildflowers and clover. "It's softer than regular hay, softer than straw, and the best bedding Gracie could hope for."

Mason helped M carry grass hay to Gracie's stall until I told them to stop. And that wasn't until it was two feet high.

"Stable-Mart uses wood shavings," I explained as I took care of Nickers' stall. My horse doesn't spend much time in the barn though. She'd rather be outside, even in a blizzard.

"Yuck!" Mason said.

"You're right, Mason!" I agreed. "Wood shavings are yucky! They may look good and be easy to muck out, but they're dangerous if a horse is sick. Horses can lie down and breathe in that wood dust and never get it out of their systems." I stopped short of telling him that foals can die from junk their moms eat or inhale. I'd told Spidells that when I worked there, but they wouldn't listen.

We exercised Gracie. I thought it would be fine to put Mason on her back since he's as light as a saddle. But I didn't want to do it without asking Madeline. And I didn't feel like asking her.

When Madeline left with Mason, M took off too.

I escaped with a ride on Nickers before it got too dark. We cantered down my favorite country lane, and I imagined we were the only two creatures on earth. Sometimes I believe that if I could end every day like this, cantering with my horse on a country lane, nothing would ever go wrong.

The rest of the night I got caught up on most of my homework. The only thing I skipped was some busywork for Pat Haven's class, life science. She'd taken over for the real teacher, who had left to "find himself" before the first day of class. Usually Pat's assignments were cool. I'd written about horses half a dozen times already. But this time she was making us look

up the fancy names for animals and their classifi-
cations. Boring. Still, I would have done it if I
hadn't been so tied up with Gracie.

Pat would understand.

*O*ne great thing about winter is that nobody expects you to ride your bike to school. *My* bike is a backward bike, invented by my dad. You pedal backward to make it go forward. No matter how often I ride it, people don't seem to get used to the sight.

Sometimes Dad drops us off in the cattle truck, which gets almost as many stares as the back bike. But on Monday I set out on foot as early as Lizzy did.

My sister has always had the reputation of being early to school—in Wyoming, through all the *I* states, and in Ashland Elementary. It was a reputation I'd never earned.

But Monday I wanted to talk to Pat before classes started. I found her reading papers in her first-period classroom. I dragged a chair to her desk and told her all about my gift horse and the colt and what the vet had said. She listened so hard, her eyes narrowed to brown lines.

"Two gift horses!" she exclaimed when I stopped for breath. "Hot dog! No offense. Reminds me of the time Mr. Haven, a fine horse trader himself, bought a Quarter Horse mare at the Ashland Auction. He set that mare in the pasture—your very pasture—that night. Next day we woke to two—mama and baby! The old horse trader who'd auctioned that mare got wind of what happened. He nearly had a cow himself! No offense. Tried to say he was hood-winked! But folks knew better. That man of mine was the most honest soul on God's green earth."

I pictured the horses in the pasture. We'd rented our house sight unseen from Pat Haven and were surprised to find the barn and pasture went with it. Even though her husband, the horse trader, died 10 years ago, the barn hadn't needed much more than a good cleaning.

Then I asked her what I'd really come to ask. "Pat, do you think the mare will be okay? And the foal?"

She glanced at me sideways. "What's your daddy say?"

"That I should toss her to the animal-control people. Or let the vet handle it. At least he's not making me do it." I felt a sharp pang of longing for my barn. How was I ever going to make it through a whole day at school without checking on Gracie?

Kids streamed into the room, bumping each other like wild Mustangs. A warning bell rang. Somebody laughed.

"I reckon you ought to skedaddle to class, Winnie," Pat said, getting up.

I got up to leave . . . without the answer I'd come for. I tore down the hall. The last thing I needed was to be late to English again.

"Walk please, Miss Willis!" hollered the principal.

I walked, which made me three seconds late to Ms. Brumby's room.

Ms. Brumby was standing at the door, as if she'd known I'd be late. Her frizzy hair was pulled back with a navy hair ribbon that matched her long skirt and jacket, shoes and purse—as if it had snowed navy.

I considered telling her I liked her *black* shoes,

which of course were navy like everything else. But even I couldn't do that to her. I leaned over to Barker and whispered, "What if Ms. Brumby woke up one morning color-blind? She'd never survive."

Barker chuckled, even though you could tell he tried not to. He's way too nice to even think about people getting smitten with color blindness.

"Attention, class!" Ms. Brumby commanded. She reminds me of the Brumby horse, a bony, Roman-nosed, Australian scrub horse. Makes me wonder how she got the name in the first place.

Brian and a couple other kids in the popular herd were in the middle of an ink fight. They didn't stop until Summer shushed them. Something was up.

"This morning," Ms. Brumby announced, crossing one navy high heel over the other as she leaned against her desk, "I have agreed to give your class president a few minutes to speak with you."

I turned to Barker. "Class president?"

Barker shrugged. "Beats me."

Then Summer Spidell strode to the front like a queen on red carpet.

"Who elected her president?" Kaylee whispered, wrinkling her tiny nose. Kaylee reminds me of another desert horse, totally different from the Brumby—the Akhal Teke, a small, compact horse with an elegant head. The Akhal Teke is fast, strong, and reliable. Although I don't know Kaylee very well, I like her. She looks like she grew up in China, but her English is a hundred times better than mine.

"Whatever happened to democracy?" I whispered back. Just like in Mustang herds, there's always one dominant female who bosses everybody around.

Ms. Brumby sat down, and Summer took over. "Some of you are disappointing me." She actually stuck out her bottom lip in a pout. "Just look at this gorgeous paper you get the privilege of selling!" She held up the swatches of wrapping paper. "We're doing the community a service! Who doesn't need wrapping paper at Christmas?"

I thought about raising my hand, since we had plenty of comics in stock at our house. But I didn't feel like explaining that to Summer.

"*I've* already sold all 20 of my rolls and am well into my second set of 20." Summer paused, as if expecting applause. "Grant sold 18."

"Go, Grant!" Brian yelled.

I smiled at Grant, who, red-faced, smiled back. He's not so bad. I wondered how his horse, Eager Star, was doing. Several months back I'd helped train the Quarter Horse for barrel races.

"Anybody want to buy some of *my* wrapping paper?" Sal asked. Her red hair had a green streak in it that matched her green-striped sweater. Earrings climbed up both of her ears like silver steps.

"Put me down for one!" Brian yelled, smiling at Sal. Brian is probably cute, if you can get past his personality.

"That is so tight!" Sal exclaimed, reaching over and mussing Brian's sandy blond hair. She turned to Summer. "Now you can't accuse me of not selling anything."

"That's fine," Summer said, glaring at me. "Because *some* people haven't sold even one piece of paper."

I met her glare until she looked away.

Kaylee leaned over and said quietly, "That wrapping paper is so expensive! I wouldn't dare ask my parents or grandparents to buy any."

"You said it! I haven't even picked mine up yet," I admitted.

"I still don't get why we have to sell this junk," a guy next to Brian complained. Everybody calls him Flash, and I couldn't remember his real name. "Why don't we just buy our own Cedar Point tickets and go?"

"You'll have to talk to Ms. Brumby about that," Summer said, glancing at our teacher.

Ms. Brumby stood beside her desk. "I explained when I agreed to help sponsor the trip. We must impose hardship on no one. Affordable for all."

"Those tickets cost 30 or 40 dollars!" Kaylee whispered.

"You're kidding!" I said back. I knew they were expensive, so expensive that Lizzy and I had never even asked Dad about it. It would be fun to go there. Going with my class was probably the only way I'd get there too. Maybe I should at least try to sell some paper.

"I sold 11 rolls!"

"I sold nine, and I think I can get rid of six more tonight!"

"I sold six, but I was sick all weekend!"

They were all girls from Summer's herd, all trying to please the dominant mare.

"Good!" Summer exclaimed. "I want everybody to think Mantis and Magnum XL-200! Think Raptor and Demon Drop!" She paused for effect. "Think Wicked Twister! All the great rides."

"Go, Summer!" came the cry.

"So your assignment is to sell at least five rolls of paper by tomorrow! And that's an order!" She did her pouty-lip thing again. "And if you let me down, fellow classmates, I'll never be able to show my face in Ms. Brumby's room again."

Note to self: Let Summer down.

I thought English class would never end. The whole morning dragged. All I could think about was Gracie, home alone.

Life science was my last class before lunch. I was so worked up over Gracie that I knew I'd never be able to eat or even sit through another class.

I slid into Pat's room and went straight to the board, where she was writing long, fancy names for animal groupings. "Pat, do you care if I go home and check on Gracie? Please? Dad's in Mansfield all day picking up supplies. Gracie could be lying there alone, sick!"

Pat stopped writing. "Well, I reckon. Just this once. If it's okay with the principal—"

"Thanks, Pat! You're the best!" I was already putting on my coat.

"But we're reviewing for the final. You be sure to get Barker's notes."

I was halfway out of the room. "Thanks!"

"Check with the principal! And you owe me today's assignment!" she called after me.

Gracie was okay, but her eyes looked empty. Her ears lopped as she paced her stall. I had to wonder if she was closer to foaling than I'd thought.

I ran to the house and came back with a bag of carrots, which I shared with Nickers and Gracie.

By the time I made it back to school, lunch period was almost over. The cafetorium, which is what they called the combination cafeteria and auditorium, smelled like grease, hot dogs, and sweat. I elbowed through throngs of kids to Catman and M's table and sat across from them.

"Have a hot dog, M," I teased, pointing to the four dogs arranged on his tray in the shape of an *M*.

"He's had nine," Catman explained. "Dude's going for the record."

Kids gawked.

Sal shouted over from Summer's table, "Go, M!"

"That is so gross!" Summer shuddered. "I hate hot dogs."

"Which makes M have to eat more just to take up your slack," I threw in.

M held each dog with thumb and forefinger and lowered it into his mouth, like a bird feeding its baby. I think he swallowed the last one whole. The crowd cheered.

After school I raced home, checked on Gracie . . . and Nickers . . . and walked back to Pat's Pets. Barker was finishing up his e-mail answers on the Pet Help Line. I read over his shoulder:

> Dear Barker,
>   Help! I think i got a mean dog from the pet shop. Every time i get near him, he growls, puts his ears back, and the hairs on his neck stand up. Should i take him back?
> —Dogman

Dear Dogman,

   Your pet is worried, not mean. Ears back and growling could be aggression. And if your dog shows his teeth and opens his mouth, then look out! But with the neck hairs raised, he's just saying, "What's wrong? Are you trying to hurt me?" So he won't be afraid of *you*, don't grab him. Let him come to you. Then pat his chest, not his head. And congratulations on your new best friend!
—Barker

I pulled up a chair as Barker answered his last e-mail:

Dear Barker,

   My dog, Sophie, keeps having run-ins with skunks. Mom won't let her back in the house until Sophie quits stinking. Can you help?
—Skunk-hater

Dear Skunk-hater,

   Here's my favorite recipe for turning your stinker back into your sweet

Sophie: 1 quart of 3% hydrogen peroxide; 1/4 cup baking soda; a tsp. of liquid soap. Get your dog all wet. Then work the skunk shampoo through her hair. Leave it on 3 or 4 minutes, then rinse. And try to get your Sophie a better playmate!
—Barker

I answered four horse questions, but they didn't seem very important compared to Gracie's problems. One girl wanted help convincing her mother it wasn't dangerous to ride bareback. Another one wanted ideas on a good name for a Palomino. And two questions got the same answers—give your horse more pasture time.

As soon as I finished with the e-mails, I logged off and started doing a little research on foals and broodmares. One site listed everything that could possibly go wrong in a horse birthing. I couldn't even finish reading it.

Pat scurried over from behind the counter. "Winnie, I plumb near forgot. It came!"

I turned around. "What came?"

"*It!*" Pat glanced around the store as if we were talking about sneaking in endangered species. "Lizzy's terrarium! It's a beauty! Want to go see? It's out back."

Lizzy's terrarium! I'd forgotten all about it. I still had enough to pay for it, but I figured I'd better wait until I found out how much I owed the vet. "Thanks, Pat. I'll have to wait. I better get back to Gracie."

M was already in the barn, rubbing down Gracie's stall with cleanser, like I'd shown him. We finished with Gracie's stall, and M followed me into Nickers'. My horse knew I needed to muck, so she kindly stepped out into the paddock.

"So how did you get to know so much about horses?" M asked, picking up Nelson.

Before I knew it, I was telling M all about my mom. It was weird. I kept talking and talking, telling stories about horses she'd gentled, about mares we'd seen foal. I guess M didn't talk, didn't keep asking me questions out loud, but I felt like I was answering them all the same.

As I talked about Mom, I felt that familiar stab in my chest. But as much as it hurt to talk about her, it also felt good to remember, to picture her and know she was still a part of my life. I wondered if that's what Ralph's prophet guy was warning Mary about, that her heart would hurt and feel good at the same time.

When Lizzy was little, she used to talk about good hurt and bad hurt. Bad hurt was falling off her bike and skinning her knee. Good hurt was getting a splinter taken out or feeling the sting of antiseptic.

"My dad didn't have anything to do with Mom's horse business in Wyoming," I continued. "I was pretty sure he didn't even like horses. That's why it was really something when he came up with the idea for me to be Winnie the Horse Gentler here. I thought he was starting to like Nickers and appreciate the other horses I worked with. Now I don't know."

When I finally shut up, M nodded, as if I'd answered all his questions. I studied his face, which was too wrinkled for an eighth-grader, his black ponytail, his black eyes that let me see myself in them. My mom would have liked M.

He walked out of Nickers' stall and back to

Gracie and rested his head against her side. "Hey, small horse. I'm M. How's it going in there? We're out here getting ready for your coming-out party. But you take all the time you need. We'll be right here."

"Cookies!" Lizzy swept into the barn with an aluminum-foil-covered plate. The warm, sweet aroma mixed with the great smells of hay and horse.

"I'm starving, Lizzy!" I shouted. "What kind of cookies?"

"Hot-dog cookies!" she exclaimed.

Nickers snorted. I did the same. I'd tried Lizzy's oatmeal pie, tuna squares, beef candy, and peanut-butter-and-jelly, three-layer cake. But I have my limits. "Elizabeth Willis, that sounds totally—"

"—creative," M finished. He lifted the foil and sniffed. "Definitely hot dog."

"Geri said that Steven said that his brother said Catman said you liked hot dogs." My sister was talking trotter speed. "But it's not all that creative. True, I may be the first to develop an edible hot-dog cookie. But Geri told me about this place called Mad Martha's on Martha's Vineyard in Massachusetts or one of those old states, which is where Geri got to go visit her aunt who has all this money, even though the rest of the family doesn't. Anyway, Mad Martha's had hot-dog ice cream on the menu! Geri didn't try it, so we don't know if it was any good."

M ended up eating four cookies on the spot and taking the rest home with him.

Tuesday after school, Catman took a turn at helping me exercise Gracie. He loved leading the mare outside in the cold of the paddock. He would have kept it up for hours if I hadn't stopped him.

Wednesday both M and Catman came over after school. We trimmed Gracie's hooves and gave her a horse massage.

In the evening, we stopped over at Barkers' to check on the puppies. Granny, Mr. and Mrs. Barker, Barker, Matthew, Mark, Luke, Johnny, and William were all decorating the biggest Christmas tree I'd ever seen. I didn't have to touch it to know it was real. The whole house smelled like pine.

Mrs. Barker brought out Christmas cookies, which Catman and M downed in two minutes, while Macho, Johnny's black-and-tan hunting dog, watched, his tail thumping the wood floor in time to the Christmas music piped through the house. Luke's Chihuahua yapped, while Matthew and his bulldog, Bull, frowned at the little white dog.

Just being inside the Barkers' house felt like Christmas, as if they loved each other so much it spilled over and got into the furniture and stove and everything else in the house.

Granny B had a story for every ornament she hung on the tree, and every story embarrassed one of the Barker boys.

M stared at a tiny nativity ornament, picturing Mary and Joseph and baby Jesus in the stable. "Nice-looking baby," he commented.

Granny Barker stared at the ornament with him.

"Did you see my Christmas bulletin on the Pet Help Line homepage?" Barker asked, standing on a stool to hang Matthew's old baby shoe on a high branch.

"Extremely cool!" Catman said, stringing a gold cord where Mrs. Barker pointed.

"What?" I asked, struck with a pang of guilt that I hadn't answered the horse e-mail in a couple of days.

"I made a dog lover's Christmas list on how to dog-proof your house at Christmas. You know—like no tinsel."

"It's metal!" Matthew added, glaring at me as if I'd dared to bring tinsel into his house. "Tinsel can mess up a dog's insides. And cover your tree water with foil!"

Barker got down from his stool. "And warnings about Christmas-light cords and berries on string, things dogs could chew. And no English holly, amaryllis, or mistletoe."

"They're poison to dogs!" Matthew declared, petting Bull.

M had disappeared. I glanced around the room.

"Puppies," Catman said, as if reading my mind and telling me where M would be. He headed down the back hallway, and I trailed after him.

Mark scurried after me. *"My* dogs are growing fast," he said.

Poor Mr. and Mrs. Barker still had a fight on their hands.

We found M lying on his back, with all four puppies crawling over him. The biggest one was chewing on M's ponytail. Two of the others were licking his face.

Catman and I played with them, too. And for almost an hour I forgot about everything that was going wrong with Christmas.

On Thursday, Mason helped M and Catman and me pile fresh grass hay in Gracie's stall. We let Mason, secure in his cowboy boots and riding helmet, sit on Gracie's back while we led her up and down the stallway. M was the one who got Madeline to give us the okay.

When we finished, M held Mason up and let him press his ear against Gracie's belly.

Mason giggled, and his thick-lensed glasses scooted down his nose. "Is it hard for a mommy horse to have a baby?" he asked, his voice soft as a horse's muzzle.

"Easier than it is on cows," I answered truthfully. I didn't add that if something does go wrong with a mare in foal, it's almost always serious, a lot more dangerous than with cows.

"I love Gracie and her baby," Mason said, trying to wrap his thin arms around the horse.

God, please don't let Mason get hurt. Make everything go okay. I'd been thinking it, and then I was praying it. God and I had come a long way since I'd moved to Ashland. For a time after Mom died, I refused to talk to God, much less listen to him. But praying was getting more natural, even automatic sometimes. I had a long way to go before I prayed like Lizzy or our mom, though.

Mason was staring at Gracie's gray-dappled splotches.

"Will you help me make a first-aid kit, Mason?" I asked, not wanting him to go away to the secret place in his mind. I knew Madeline still hated it when Mason followed us to the barn. But I also knew it wasn't because she thought we couldn't take care of him. She didn't want her son to get too attached to the mare.

It was too late for that.

Mason brought out towels from the supply room. I gathered clean strips of cloth, string, scissors, a squeeze bottle, iodine, soap, bandages, and plastic sleeves, which are like big gloves. We packed everything into a small suitcase I'd brought from Wyoming. I could hardly wait for school to be out for Christmas so Dad would let me start spending nights in the barn.

There were more reasons why I couldn't wait to get out of school. Summer had made a sales chart and posted it big as life in Ms. Brumby's room. Each day we had to record how many rolls of wrapping paper we'd sold. I tried not to let it bother me, but I was the only one with all zeros.

Just to get Summer off my back, I decided I'd try to sell a couple of rolls. Then, if we really did raise enough money to go to Cedar Point, I wouldn't have to feel guilty.

On Friday I stomped snow off my boots and headed straight for Pat's class before school.

She acted glad to see me. "Winnie! I was just

praying for you and that horse. Did you come by to bring me those assignments?"

I couldn't believe I'd forgotten about them . . . again. I shook my head. I should have done them. And I should have gotten Barker's notes too.

I changed the subject. "Pat, our class is selling Christmas wrapping paper. Would you—?"

She laughed. " 'Fraid you're barking up the wrong tree, no offense! I made that mistake already—all that money for that little bit of paper on the roll! Mighty pretty, but whoo-ee!"

"You already bought paper . . . from someone else?" I'd never even thought of that. She must have known I'd be selling too.

"Let's see here . . . Brian, Barker, and a roll from Summer. Wish I'd unrolled the paper before unrolling my bankroll."

"But I haven't even sold one single roll, Pat."

"Sorry! Must've had me a dozen or two kiddos try to sell me paper this week alone."

Kids streamed into the classroom. One of them edged between us and asked Pat something about the final.

I wandered off to Ms. Brumby's room.

Couldn't Pat have bought one roll from me? Would it have killed her?

Instead I had to trail into Ms. Brumby's room just as the bell rang and get in the "reporting line." Ahead of me, Kaylee wrote a *1* in her box. Grant wrote *6*. When it was my turn, I filled in the square the way I'd filled in every other square—with a big fat goose egg. No offense.

$\mathcal{S}$aturday night Hawk called from Florida. As soon as I heard her voice, I wanted to say a million things—that I missed her, that Mason and Nickers and I missed Towaco, that I wished she'd come home and help me with Gracie.

Instead I said, "Hi, Hawk. Having a good time?"

"I miss Peter Lory," she said. "He would love this balcony." Peter Lory is her favorite bird, a red chattering lory she named after an old actor, Peter Lorre. I've never seen him, but Hawk loves him in black-and-white crime movies.

"How's Towaco?" I asked, imagining the Appy with a Florida sunburn.

"Towaco and I prefer Ohio," Hawk admitted.

I tried to fight feeling happy about that. But as soon as I'd stopped worrying about her trailer in the snowstorm, I'd started worrying that she'd love Florida and want to stay there. I was glad she liked cold, snowy Ohio better.

Neither of us said anything. I could hear her breathing and birds chirping out on the balcony.

Finally Hawk asked, "How are you, Winnie?"

I started to say fine. I'd played it safe with Hawk since the first time we met, when she was known only as Victoria Hawkins. She'd been guarded too. But we'd started breaking through that stuff. It was no time to go backward. "Not so good."

"Tell me everything," Hawk said.

So I did. I told her about my gift horse and the mysterious *Topsy-Turvy-Double-U*. I told her about what the vet said and how Dad was acting, never missing an opportunity to remind me that Gracie wouldn't make it. I talked about Mason and how he was getting attached to the mare.

Suddenly I glanced at the kitchen clock. "Hawk, I'm sorry! You're paying for long distance!"

"Dad can afford it," she said.

She was right about that. "I should be asking about *you,* Hawk. Have you talked to your mom? What are kids like down there? When are you showing Towaco? You guys will win everything, you know."

She answered all my questions, talking a lot for Hawk. Then she got quiet, so quiet I thought she might have gotten disconnected. "Winnie, I wish I were home. Ashland home. I wish I could be there to help you with Gracie." She gave me her Florida phone number. "And call me if Gracie has her foal. Promise?"

I promised.

When I hung up, I felt better than I had in days . . . until I remembered that I still didn't have a Christmas present for Hawk. With less than a week till Christmas, I had to admit there was no way I could afford everything I wanted to buy—especially the terrarium *and* a subscription to *Gizmo Magazine.* I'd had to buy high-energy feed, mineral supplement, and protein supplement, which had cut deep into my shrinking Christmas funds. Plus, there was still the vet bill to worry about since I'd promised Dad I could cover it.

Sunday after church I took a long ride on
Nickers, then spent the rest of the day with
Catman and M, mucking and laying straw.

By the time I finally dragged myself in from the
barn, it was pitch-dark. Lizzy and Geri were at the
kitchen table, which was covered in piles of rocks
and construction paper. Cookie smell smothered
every other house odor. A dozen paper plates full
of cookies, covered in plastic wrap and tied with
red ribbons, lined the counter.

"Where are you taking cookies?" I asked,
shedding my hat and coat. My hair was flat and
damp with sweat. Lizzy's hair looked perfect,
falling in little curls around her shoulders. Geri's
blonde hair did the same thing. They both had
on pajamas, so I figured Geri was spending the
night again. She did it a lot when her parents
worked night shift at the Archway Cookie
factory, but she didn't usually stay over on
school nights. Maybe it was because we only
had a three-day week ahead.

"Good Shepherd Nursing Home," Lizzy
answered.

"We made only soft cookies," Geri added. "No nuts in case of no teeth."

I glanced around the house for Dad and noticed the Christmas decorations everywhere. Red and green paper chains dangled above windows. Lizzy and Geri had made Christmas candles and papier-mâché trees and angels. She'd even talked Dad into buying a tiny Christmas tree at the grocery store and then decorated it with cookies and strung popcorn.

I'd missed it all.

"House looks nice, Lizzy," I said, trying not to feel too guilty for not helping with any of it. "Where's Dad?"

Lizzy had the end of a paintbrush in her mouth and both hands occupied with one of the rocks. So Geri answered. "Your dad took Madeline and Mason for last-minute Christmas shopping."

Last-minute shopping? I hadn't done *any* shopping.

I sat down at the table with them. Geri was folding green paper, and Lizzy was painting on a rock the size of my fist. "I thought this would be my best Christmas for giving presents," I admitted. "It's the first time I've had money of my own . . . *had* money of my own. Gracie's taking most of it. I'm going to have to settle for buying junk from A-Mart."

Lizzy spit out the paintbrush. "You can *make* your gifts, Winnie! There's still time! We can help you. Right, Geri?"

Geri nodded. "Sure. Here you go." She handed me a small green square of paper. "I'm making Christmas doves for my aunts. See?" She held up seven green origami birds with yarn loops on their backs. "Tree ornaments!"

"Nice," I said, wondering if doves were green and how they'd show up on a Christmas tree. I was getting itchy to leave. I hate crafts. Probably because I stink at them. Even if Geri were folding paper horses, I knew I didn't have a chance of success here.

"Now," Geri commanded, "do what I do. Fold it like this." She made a fold and smoothed it out. I did the same. "Good. Only match your edges. Okay. Now this way."

She folded triangles. She creased hexagons.

When we finished, she held hers up. "There! See! Nothing to it—and it's beautiful frog green!" She took mine out of my palm and frowned at it. It looked like a green paper clip with wrinkles.

Before Geri could comment, Lizzy spit out her paintbrush. "Hey! I've got some extra rocks. Want to paint—?"

"Thanks, Lizzy." I got up. My chair squeaked against the kitchen linoleum. "Maybe tomorrow."

But I didn't mean it. I knew full well I'd be worse at painting rocks than I'd been at folding doves.

But Monday morning Lizzy was waiting with her rocks and Geri with her construction paper. "Winnie!" Lizzy cried when I stumbled out of our room before the sun had time to even think about rising.

I'd lost track of how many night trips I'd made to the barn to check on Gracie. But judging from how hard it was to keep my eyes open, it must have been a lot. I'd get more sleep when I could just stay out in the barn.

"We have time to get started on a Christmas rock before school!" Lizzy exclaimed.

"Or try origami again," Geri offered.

I tried to walk past them to the bathroom, but Lizzy shoved a pencil at me. "Here! Take this.

You can draw your design now. Then after school we can mix paints and—"

"I can't even see the pencil now, Lizzy." I yawned. "And I've got to check on Gracie. I want to slip in a quick ride on Nickers too. Later, okay?"

After school there she was again. And so was Geri. I made excuses for not rock-painting. I'd had another lousy day. Pat had caught me in the hall and nagged for the assignments I hadn't turned in. Summer had been . . . Summer. And I still hadn't gotten Barker's notes for the life-science final.

Tuesday was just as bad. Summer was even more obnoxious, and I kept getting further behind in Pat's class.

After school I walked straight home. But before I'd even gotten into the house, Dad cornered me on the lawn. He was working on a remote-controlled stapler, and his hands were full of copper wires and staples. But he still had time to remind me that Gracie wasn't looking good and I had to be prepared for what was going to happen, meaning death.

The rest of the day I successfully dodged Lizzy and Geri. The last thing I needed was crafts. I didn't even like the sound of the word. I knew Lizzy was trying to help, but she didn't get it. She can do everything great. And every time she tried to get me to paint those stupid rocks, I felt even more pressure about the Christmas gifts I didn't have.

I kept telling myself that I only had one more day of classes to get through. Then Dad would let me stay in the barn. And I'd have enough time to take the money I had left and buy something—even if it wouldn't be something great—for Christmas gifts.

Wednesday was the last day of school before Christmas break. All I wanted to do was get it over with. I was almost out of the house, headed for morning barn chores, when Lizzy surprised me.

"Winnie! Geri and I went through a bunch of craft books last night. We found six designs you can trace right on the rocks! And if you choose one, I could even trace it for you because that wouldn't be like me doing it or anything. And then—"

"Lizzy!" I couldn't take it anymore. Not one more job. Not even if they did everything for me but sign my name. "I'm not a craft person! Can't you and your little friend get that through your heads?"

I ran outside. The cold slapped my cheeks. I'd forgotten to pull on my stocking cap. My head felt prickly. And my whole insides hurt.

I dashed into the barn, my favorite place in the world. But it didn't feel right. The warmth felt scratchy. It melted my frozen head, and tears streamed down my cheeks.

Nickers greeted me like always, nickering and burrowing her head into my chest. I wrapped my arms around her and tried to stop crying. I wanted my mother. It made me feel five years old, but I wanted her. I didn't want to go through another Christmas—or another day— without her.

I made myself go through the motions of barn chores. I tried not to think about how I'd blown up at Lizzy, but it was all I could think about.

Lizzy was only trying to help me. She was always trying to help me—when she wasn't delivering cookies to old people in nursing homes or helping injured reptiles. *I love my sister. Don't let her feel bad.* I realized I was talking to God now, not to myself. I could almost feel him in the stall with me. *I'm sorry. I just wanted to get such great Christmas gifts. And I can't make them. Not like Lizzy and Geri. So make it better, please? Make me better?*

I put down the last armful of clean straw and knew what I had to do, what I wanted to do. I raced back to the house, faster than I'd run out of it. "Lizzy! Lizzy, I'm sorry!"

But nothing came back to me except my own words.

Lizzy was gone.

*W*hat I wanted to do was go straight to Ashland Elementary, march into Lizzy's class-room, and tell her how sorry I was. But I couldn't be late for English again.

One more day. I kept repeating it as my boots crunched the snow. I needed school to be out. I needed to see my sister and make things right again.

Halfway down the hall to English, I heard Pat holler from her classroom, "Winnie!"

I still didn't have her assignments. I hadn't gotten notes from Barker. And today was the life-science final. "I'm in a hurry," I told her, stopping, but not walking back to her.

"You okay?" she hollered.

A couple of kids turned to look at Pat, then

at me. I traipsed back to her door so the whole school wouldn't hear us. "I guess."

"Well, I hope you're set for the final today, Winnie. Your dad was so proud of that mid-term A!"

At least he had that. I shrugged.

Summer had already taken her spot at the front of Ms. Brumby's class when I got there. Great. Another pep talk, and I still had nothing but goose eggs by my name.

Ms. Brumby, head-to-toe yellow, waved her grade book at us to quiet us down. "I don't think your essay test should take the whole period, so I've agreed to give Summer one last 'commercial break' for your wrapping-paper project."

I groaned.

Barker leaned over from his seat next to me. "Winnie, are you okay?"

I should have felt grateful that he cared enough to ask. I managed a smile and a nod. But what I was thinking was that I didn't have a gift for Barker. And I'd spotted one under his tree for me, along with Catman's and Lizzy's.

Summer started off by praising everybody who had sold 20 or more rolls of paper. Most of them were her friends anyway.

I sat on the front row and glared at her, wishing I had blown up at Summer instead of Lizzy.

She glanced at me from time to time, probably feeling the heat of my stare. "Most of you have at least *tried* to help out." She pointed to her wall chart. "I am just so proud of those of you with gold stars by your name."

"Oh, brother," I mumbled.

"Did you have a question, Winifred?" Summer asked, turning her fake smile on me.

"No," I answered firmly.

"Because if there's some problem, perhaps we can help." Summer made a sweeping gesture with the hand that wasn't holding wrapping paper.

I continued to glare at her. If I'd been a horse, my ears would have been flat back, and my teeth would have been bared.

Summer shook her head slowly, her eyes wide with fake concern. "I admit I don't understand why you couldn't sell at least one roll of wrapping paper. I mean, you of all people should be trying your hardest."

Barker's chair squeaked. "Shouldn't we start taking our test?" he asked.

"Good idea!" Kaylee seconded.

"Me of all people?" I repeated, the veins in

my neck pulsing as I sat up straighter. "Why *me of all people?*"

Summer smiled down at me, like a queen to her poor, deformed subject. "You and your kind are the reason we're having this sale."

I almost wished Summer's little crowd would have laughed. That they didn't, that they maybe felt sorry for me, was worse. I was someone you feel sorry for.

I didn't hear things after that. I think Barker said something. Summer and Ms. Brumby said things. I couldn't take in Ms. Brumby's instructions as she passed out our final. I remember reading the questions, writing answers.

Summer's was the voice I heard ringing in my ears long after I'd turned in my paper and left the classroom. *You of all people . . . you and your kind.*

I moved around from class to class, sitting in the right seat, leaving when the bell rang. Pat Haven passed out our life-science final. I tried to read the questions, but the words wouldn't stay on the page. My brain was wrapped around *you and your kind.* Some of the questions I didn't even try to answer. Who would expect *you and your kind* to do well on a final anyway?

I must have eaten lunch, must have finished afternoon classes. And then I was walking home, faster and faster, slipping on the icy edges of pavement. I broke into a run when I turned onto our street.

Dad's truck was parked at the curb. I was glad. I wanted him to be home. I wanted to ask him about *you and your kind*. Was *he* part of it? Who else was *our kind*? Why didn't I know it before?

I stumbled across our lawn, tripping over mangled toasters that never got repaired, spools of wire and old tires, washing-machine motors, parts waiting to be invented.

I remembered running home another day after school—in Wyoming, maybe second grade. Some kid—Benji or Bradley maybe—had called me Annie Oakley. I hadn't known what it meant, but the way the kid said it made me feel awful, like I was feeling now. I'd burst into the house and exploded into tears. My mom had listened to everything and said, "Why, Winnie, we should phone that young man right now and thank him! Annie Oakley was a hero and a legend." And we did. We phoned him. And everything was safe again.

I threw open the door, wanting to tell my dad

everything Summer had said. I wanted to have him make it okay to be *you and your kind.*

"Dad!" I shut the door and tore off my coat. "Dad?"

Dad came in from the living room. "Good. You're home." But his eyes didn't say *good.* His forehead was wrinkled, and he looked shriveled, like someone had let the air out of him.

I started to tell him anyway. "Dad, at school—"

He held out an envelope with a window in it. "This came. It was addressed to me."

I took it. It was from the vet. I unfolded the bill. Sixty-eight dollars. Dr. Stutzman had sent the blood sample to the lab. Gracie was pregnant. And I owed $68.

I swallowed hard. "I-I've got it, Dad. I told you I could pay it out of Towaco's fees." And I could, although I'd have to borrow a little from next month's hay budget. And my Christmas fund was totally wiped out. "It's okay. Really."

"I know you believe you're doing the right thing for this horse, Winnie," Dad said. I braced myself. "And I respect you for that. You have a good heart. It's just . . . this doesn't change things. You have to remember what Dr. Stutzman said about that horse. She's not going to make it. You can't set your heart on every-thing turning out the way you want it to just because that's the way you want it. Otherwise, your heart's going to be broken."

I nodded, pulled my coat back on, stuffed the bill into my pocket, and went back outside.

Halfway to the barn, I saw Geri's mom's car turn onto our street. I don't know why, but I ducked behind the trunk of a big oak and watched the car pull in front of our house. The back door opened, and Lizzy hopped out, laugh-ing. I could hear Geri and her mother laughing too.

Lizzy looked so pretty, her hair flowing from under a little beret she'd found in a garage sale. She leaned into the backseat and said some-thing, then stood up and waved.

I dashed to the barn, praying she hadn't seen me. There was no way Lizzy was part of *you and your kind*. She would have sold more rolls of paper than anybody if she'd been in my class. Everybody wanted to be like Lizzy. I felt like I had to, for Lizzy's sake, stay away from her. If I didn't, I could contaminate her, make her part of *my kind*.

I hurried through the barn and almost tripped over Nelson. Stumbling, I kept going to Gracie's stall. I had to keep myself together. Gracie was counting on me. The foal needed me. I had to put Summer out of my head. This was my barn, where everything always got back to normal for me. It would be okay. The worst was over. No more school until after New Year's. And by then, I'd show everybody, even Dad and Dr. Stutzman. Gracie would be fine, and she'd have a healthy, normal foal.

I stopped cold outside Gracie's stall. Something wasn't right.

At first I didn't know what was wrong. She drooped. Her ears lopped, but they'd been like that since she'd shown up in the pasture.

Then I saw it. She was dripping milk.

It was too soon. She wasn't ready to foal. And I didn't like the look of the milk, thin and weak, coming out too fast.

I collapsed to the dirt, drew up my knees, and burst into tears.

I sat in the stallway outside Gracie's stall and sobbed. Even when I heard Nickers whinny at me, I didn't look up.

"Winnie?" Lizzy ran through the barn, knelt beside me, and wrapped her arms around me. "What's the matter? I was coming out to get you. Then I heard this noise, and it was you crying. And I couldn't believe it. Are you okay? What happened? Is it Gracie?" She stood up and gazed through the stall at the mare. "I can't tell, Winnie! Is she . . . is she worse?"

I tried to stop crying, but my sides heaved, making me gasp for breath. "Sh-she's . . . losing her milk. And . . . it's too soon. And I owe too much money to the vet. And . . . I was so mean to you, Lizzy." I broke down all over again,

133

recalling the way I'd snapped at her when she was only trying to do me a favor.

I felt Lizzy's arms around me again, her head on my head. "Winnie, it's okay. It's all okay."

"No it's not!" I cried. "You were just trying to help me! And I'm so stupid I can't even fold a green dove."

Lizzy laughed. Something in it reminded me of our mother's laugh. Chills ran down my arms and legs. "Well, that does explain why you're so upset," she said. "I would be, too, if I couldn't fold a green dove."

I glanced up at her. "I'm so sorry, Lizzy. I could make a million excuses, but I won't. I'm just sorry. Okay?"

"More than okay." She pulled off her scarf and used it to wipe my face. "Rotten day, huh?"

"You don't know the half of it." I grinned at her as she dabbed my cheeks with her scarf, her eyes set like she was painting or figuring something out. "You remind me so much of Mom," I said quietly.

Lizzy blinked. "What?"

"Mom. You remind me of her."

She sat back on her heels. "How?"

"Lots of ways," I said, seeing Mom in Lizzy's

mouth, the way her forehead wrinkled, the way she held one arm with the other.

"You're the one who's like Mom," Lizzy said slowly. "Horse lovers, horse gentlers. I can't even stand to get near one."

"Not that way, Lizzy. You're like her in goodness. Inside. Like in your spirit." Mom was gentle like Lizzy. They knew Jesus better than me.

Now Lizzy was crying. "Winnie, that's the nicest thing you've ever said to me. It's the nicest thing anybody's ever said to me." She sniffed and used the scarf on herself. "It's the nicest thing anybody's ever said to anybody."

And it was my turn to hug her.

"Gracie!" I let go of Lizzy so fast, she toppled backward. "Lizzy, I have to try to save this milk. I don't know if it's good enough for the foal or not. But I need to save what I can."

"You're not going to ask me to . . . to . . . like do anything with the horse, are you?" Lizzy asked, as I went into Gracie's stall.

"I need help, Lizzy. Call Catman!"

"Good idea!"

"Then find me containers with lids—margarine bowls!"

"Got it!" Lizzy ran out.

I scratched Gracie's chest, then felt her ears to see if she was hot or cold. She seemed okay. She wasn't sick. She was just losing her first milk, something her foal would need.

I heard voices outside the barn. Then Lizzy shouted, "They're here! I didn't even have to call them!"

Catman and M appeared in the shadow of the barn.

"What's happening, man?" Catman asked, coming into the stall, with M right behind him.

M squatted and looked underneath Gracie. "She's leaking!"

"It could mean a couple of things," I said, trying to sound calmer than I felt. My hands were shaking. "It might mean she's ready to foal, but I don't think so. She's not waxing. That's when the mare is close to foaling and the milk is so thick it looks like wax. But sometimes older or sick horses lose milk before it's time. I think that's what's going on."

"Can she make more?" M asked.

"Not first milk," I explained. Mom had kept first milk in the freezer in Wyoming. And I'd used Pat's computer to double-check everything about what a foal needs.

"Colostrum." Catman was pacing like a nervous father in a TV sitcom.

"That's right," I agreed. M hadn't exactly asked, but I could feel that he wanted to know more. "Horses aren't like other animals. They're born without any antibodies, no defense against disease. The only way they get antibodies is through nursing, drinking the first milk that comes out of the mare."

"We have to do something!" M cupped his hands under the udder.

"Here they are!" Lizzy ran over and handed us five small white containers. "I had to dump margarine out of two of them. Is this all right? And I brought hot water because they always need it in the movies."

Catman took everything from her.

M was whispering to the foal.

"Thanks, Lizzy." I poured the water into one of the bowls and used liquid soap and a sponge from my first-aid kit to wash the udders.

"Can I do anything else?" Lizzy asked.

"Pray!" I hadn't even thought to pray myself. At least I had sense enough to ask Lizzy to.

"God, help Winnie do what she needs to do with this horse. And please keep that little baby horse safe." Lizzy was talking to God out loud, but it didn't feel weird. She might have been talking to Catman or M.

I caught Catman's worried gaze. It was as close as I've ever seen Catman come to being rattled. "I'm going to milk her," I explained. "We'll save it for her baby."

"I dig. Then it's all cool, right?" Catman asked.

I shook my head. "I don't know. The milk doesn't look right. It isn't thick enough. It's too white. But I'll collect it. It's all we can do for now."

M had his ear pressed to Gracie's side. He stepped back so I could get to her udders. Lizzy got as close as the stall door.

"Easy, Gracie. We're going to help you get ready for that foal." I rubbed my hands together to warm them.

Gracie craned her neck around, saying, *I hurt. Don't make me hurt more.*

I squatted on her near side, which is what you call the left side of a horse. Positioning the margarine container under her udder, I squeezed with my thumb and forefinger and pulled down gently from each side of the teat. The barn was still except for the *squirt, squirt* into the plastic bowl.

Nickers stuck her head over the stall divider and watched.

I filled the first container and handed it off to Catman. We didn't talk. Not even Lizzy. I kept milking for two more containers' worth, until her udders relaxed. Gracie groaned, a contented grunt, as if she finally had relief.

"Done." I stood up and handed the last container to M, who put on the lid.

"Is it enough?" Lizzy asked.

"Check it out, man." Catman lifted the lid and sniffed. "Smells like milk."

I felt it with my fingers. It wasn't very sticky.

M stared at the bowl. You could almost hear him wondering how we'd know if the colostrum was good enough.

"We'll test it," I said, answering his unspoken question. I turned to Lizzy. "Remember that gadget Madeline gave Dad so he could test his antifreeze?"

"The one that's supposed to double as a turkey baster?" Lizzy asked.

"Gross!" Catman said.

"No kidding," Lizzy agreed. "Madeline says she's invented the perfect disinfectant for it, too. So it's supposed to be safe for antifreeze *and* for turkey, as long as you use her cleaner. The patent people admitted she proved her case. But they couldn't get past the idea of antifreeze and turkey, so they didn't give her the patent."

"You and Dad haven't used the thing yet, right?" I asked, trying to cut to the chase.

She shook her head.

"Good! I need it." I'd seen Mom use a brand-new antifreeze kit on our broodmare's colostrum in Wyoming once.

"I know right where it is!" Lizzy shouted, running out of the barn. In minutes, she returned with the antifreeze kit.

I took the contraption out of the box and removed the wrapper.

"It sure looks like a turkey baster," Lizzy observed. "Except for the little balls inside."

I squeezed the plastic bulb on top and stuck the tube into the first container of milk. "If the balls float in the milk, we're in business. The colostrum's good enough quality, with enough vitamins and antibodies to make that foal healthy."

"And if they sink?" M asked out loud.

"Then we're sunk," I answered. "There." I took the tube, full of milk now, out of the container and held it up so we could all watch.

It didn't take long. First one ball floated to the bottom. Then another. Then another.

We stared at the milk, which was so thin only one lone ball remained afloat. Then it plunged through the swirls of white, sinking . . . sinking. And when it sank to the bottom, something inside of me sank too.

Chapter 14

I dropped the baster and watched the worthless first milk splash to the ground. Then I stroked Gracie, scratching her chest and pressing my face against her neck. "It's not your fault, Gracie," I muttered. "You're doing everything you can for your baby. We know that."

"Oh, Winnie," Lizzy murmured, not saying more.

M covered his head with his arms and turned away.

Catman stared at his container of milk. "Bummer. Major bummer."

"If it were spring," I said, thinking out loud, "there'd be mares with foals around here. We could work something out, let our foal nurse from another mare." This foal was going to need colostrum. "I'll buy it!" I blurted out.

Lizzy perked up. "Buy it? You can buy it! That rocks, Winnie! Why didn't you tell us that in the first place? So where do we go? Are there colostrum stores?"

"You can't just go to a store," I explained. "It's hard to get. Only really big stables collect it and freeze it. They have it on hand for their own horses, just in case. But if they have enough in the colostrum bank, they sell it. It costs an arm and a leg."

"Who has a colostrum bank then?" Lizzy asked. But as soon as she got her question out, her face sagged. She knew the answer. We all did.

"Spidells," M said.

Dad agreed to drive me to Spidells' Stable-Mart. He didn't say anything the whole way over. He didn't have to. I knew what he was thinking. I was wasting money I didn't have.

It didn't take long for Spider Spidell to realize he had us over a barrel. "Well," he said, when he finally came over to talk to us in the stable office, "every real equine operation needs cutting-edge technology." He was wearing a blue shirt. His stubborn rim of dark hair came to a point in back, leaving the rest of his head bald. I've always thought he looked like a blue jay. Hawk told me blue jays are one of the meanest birds out there.

"So do you have colostrum?" I repeated. Dad and I had been standing in the little office for 15 minutes, long enough to have counted the silver trophies on his shelves—63.

Mr. Spidell puffed out his chest, but it didn't puff as far as his belly did. "Colostrum is a valuable commodity in the horse industry. At Stable-Mart, we make it our business to keep a supply, should any of our clients' broodmares come up short. Yes, we make sure to foresee any liabilities which—"

"How much?" Dad asked, cutting him off.

Spider Spidell grinned. He had every right to grin. He didn't just charge me an arm and a leg; he went for the lungs, kidneys, and heart.

I took three pints of colostrum, frozen in separate plastic bags. Then I asked Mr. Spidell to bill me.

On the ride home I subtracted in my head. I wouldn't be able to pay until I got Towaco's next check for boarding. But I couldn't think about that now. The foal needed this to survive.

At home Lizzy watched as I packed the three bags of colostrum into the freezer, next to her homemade green ice cream. Dad stood at a distance and sighed, like the force of the air coming out of him was the only thing keeping the words in him.

For the next couple of days M and Catman kept Gracie and me company during the day. Nights I slept on a cot in Nickers' stall. I could peek through the slats without disturbing Gracie.

The second night, as I piled every available blanket onto the cot, Pat Haven dropped by. I hadn't seen her since the life-science final. I hadn't even been to Pat's Pets. On top of everything else, I'd been feeling like I'd lost Pat. Maybe even Pat Haven had had it with *you and your kind*.

"Hey, Winnie!" Pat called, her boots clomping on the barn floor. "Been thinking 'bout you."

"I really messed up that final, didn't I?" I asked, brushing hay off my pillow.

"It wasn't one of your shining moments," Pat

admitted. She stomped snow off her cowboy boots. "Catman's been keeping me up on Gracie's news, though. He said you slept out here all night." She was carrying a garbage bag, which she tossed to me in Nickers' stall.

I caught it, opened it, and saw a giant blanket.

"Down comforter," Pat explained. "Thought you could use it out here. Better than a heater. Call it a Christmas gift. It's been stored away in the attic since my husband passed. Oh, and I put some baby bottles in that sack—the good kind, with the lambs' nipples."

I couldn't believe she was bringing me a gift after the way I'd been lately. "Pat, I don't have any money to buy you anything, and I wanted to get you a great cowboy hat. And now I can't even buy that terrarium for Lizzy, and I've stuck you with it. Plus, I'm so far behind in the horse e-mails—"

"Gracious, Winnie! You're talking faster than Lizzy. I can't keep up! I reckon I can't think of a thing I need for Christmas any-who. And Lizzy's terrarium will keep. As for horse e-mails, they'll keep too. Barker and I have been checking them for emergencies. Not that many e-mails, what with Christmas and all."

I could feel my neck muscles unknot. "Thanks, Pat." She was still my friend, even though I'd let her down on every count.

"Well, don't be so quick to thank me until after you get your semester grade. Hey, but you got next semester to bring your grade back up, right? Life science runs the whole year. You can't get rid of me that easy!"

I liked that, that Pat was one of the people I couldn't get rid of—like Lizzy. Like *my kind*. "Pat, the other day Summer said something that kind of got to me."

Pat nodded for me to go on.

"She said our class was raising money for . . . for 'you and your kind.' "

Pat grinned and looked at me sideways. "Honey, don't you listen to talk like that. There's always going to be some pack of wolves—no offense to the wolves—ready to attack and hurt. *That's* the *kind* you don't want to be!"

I set the comforter on the cot and went out in the stallway to hug her. She felt soft and smelled like lilacs.

"You go on now," she said, her voice raspy. "Take care of that mare. We're going to have us a merry Christmas, and that's that!" She turned to go.

"Pat!" I called before she reached the barn door. "Do you think Gracie will have her foal all right?" I wanted her to say yes, to promise.

"I sure hope so, Winnie."

"But what if you hope and it doesn't come true?" I had to swallow to keep tears down.

Pat smiled at me. "Well, then you've at least hoped. And that's never a bad thing."

It wasn't good enough. Nobody could hope harder than I had. People hope for all kinds of things that never happen. And they hope for things not to happen, and they do anyway. "But it *is* a bad thing, Pat! I'm hoping like crazy Gracie and her foal will be all right. And if they're not . . ." I couldn't finish it.

"Then God will help all of us get through it." Pat fiddled with her boots, then smiled at me. "In the meantime, you go on and hope! 'Hope does not disappoint us, because God has poured out his love into our hearts.' You can take that verse to the bank!"

Two days before Christmas, a blizzard hit. The wind whistled through the barn and house. Lizzy turned up the heat in the lizard lair Dad had invented for Larry and the other lizards in my sister's Ohio collection. I stayed toasty warm all night under Pat's down comforter.

The day before Christmas I was beginning to wonder if Gracie would ever have her foal. I'd gone in the house to clean up, change clothes, and get something to eat, when Madeline and Mason dropped by.

Dad let them in and took Madeline's coat. "Don't forget about the Christmas Eve service at church tonight," he said.

"I told you we'd be there, Jack." I could have been wrong, but I thought she sounded peeved with him.

"If you want me to drive over and pick you guys up, just say the word," Dad offered.

Mason had gone straight to our little Christmas tree and was touching the tips of the pine needles.

"Want to come to the barn with me, Mason?"

I asked. I turned to Madeline. "If it's okay with your mom."

Madeline sighed. "All right. Put your gloves back on, Mason."

I carried Mason on my shoulders through calf-deep snow to the barn. He giggled the whole time, tilting back his head and sticking out his tongue to catch snowflakes. "Giddyap, horsey!" Mason shouted when I jogged the last stretch to the barn.

He was so happy around the horses. I didn't want him to end up sad. I knew that's what Madeline and Dad were worried about. I tried to remember Pat's verse about hope not disappointing us, but I couldn't.

There's something about being around Mason, like being around Nickers, that makes me feel closer to God. Maybe that's why I found myself praying. *I know tomorrow is Jesus' birthday, but I just don't feel like celebrating. Don't get me wrong—I'm really glad you came down here. I'm just too worried about Gracie. I know you're busy, this being your biggest time of the year and all. But could you please help Gracie have a healthy, happy foal?*

Gracie stopped pacing when I put Mason

down and we joined her in the stall. "I love you, horsey," Mason said, hugging Gracie's foreleg.

I picked him up so he wouldn't get stepped on by accident. "She loves you too, Mason," I said.

"But she's sick?" he asked.

"She's sick," I answered.

"Where did she live before?" he asked, squirming out of my arms so he could offer Gracie a handful of hay.

"I don't know, Mason." I hadn't thought about the owner or *Topsy-Turvy* for days. Part of me was still angry. The other part of me was glad they'd left her. I wondered if I'd ever know who sent the gift horse.

Madeline came for Mason, and they went home to finish Christmas preparations.

In the afternoon Catman and M came over, already dressed for church. Catman's paisley shirt collar poked out of his army jacket, and he'd traded in his sandals for moccasins. M, of course, wore all black, which looked speckled with hay dust and horsehair after the first 10 minutes in the barn.

Lizzy appeared late in the day. She looked

great, wearing a bright red sweater she'd picked up at Goodwill. "Everything okay out here?" she asked.

I didn't like the way Gracie had been pacing in the stall. And her eyes seemed glazed over. I shrugged. M and Catman didn't venture an answer either.

"You need to go change for church, Winnie." Lizzy turned to M and Catman as I headed out. "You two can ride with us . . . or the Barkers. Whatever you want. Barkers are coming by at seven. I hope you're really hungry. You should see what I made for the Christmas Eve potluck dinner. I hope we get to eat first and have the service after. I don't want to miss a word, and I can't keep my stomach from growling. On the other hand, if I get my solo out of the way, my stomach won't have butterflies and—"

Her voice faded as I crossed the lawn. Inside my room I changed into my long, black velvet skirt and the green blouse Lizzy had bought weeks ago at Experienced Clothes, which means secondhand. I ran a brush through my hair and hurried back to the barn.

"Winnie!" Lizzy screamed. "Come here! Fast!"

Heart pounding, I raced past my sister to Gracie's stall. M and Catman were hovered next to the mare. Catman's eyes bugged. "Winnie, something's wrong, man. Something's way wrong."

Chapter 15

I almost knocked M down getting to Gracie. She was pawing the ground, her eyes wide. Sweat dripped from her chest and behind her elbows.

"She's roasting," Catman said, pressing his palm to her forehead.

Gracie craned her head around toward her flank. Then she bit her belly.

"She's trying to hurt herself!" M cried.

"Out!" I shoved both of them out of the stall. "We can't all be here. You're making her crazy."

Gracie lifted her tail. She snatched a mouthful of hay, then pivoted and started pacing again. I kept out of her way. Suddenly she dropped to the hay. Then she stood up again.

My insides were trembling. "She's in the first

stage of delivery!" I announced, trying to keep my voice down. "Gracie's getting ready to have her foal!"

"Far out!" Catman shouted.

I shot him a look to shut him up. Catman of all people! We couldn't risk disturbing the mare.

"Man!" Catman shouted it again, then slapped his hands over his mouth.

I sneaked out of her stall just as Gracie kicked at her abdomen.

"Neat-o!" Catman cried. "Sorry, man," he whispered, but even his whisper was too loud. Half a dozen barn cats had tiptoed up to him, as if to make sure *he* was all right.

I crossed the barn to where everybody was huddled. "Lizzy, take the bags of colostrum out of the freezer and put them in the sink so they can defrost. You're going to have to tell Dad that I can't go to Christmas Eve service."

"Is she really and truly having the baby?" Lizzy whispered. "This is so perfect! Christmas Eve and—"

"Lizzy!" I stopped her. If she really got going talking, the foal would be a yearling before she finished. "Go!"

She tore out of the barn.

I turned to Catman and M. "You too."

"That's a negative. I'll stay and help, man!" Catman declared, too loud.

I had never seen the cool Catman like this. "Thanks, Catman," I said, trying to think of how diplomatic Lizzy would have handled things. "But Ralph will be so disappointed if you're not at the Christmas Eve service. Remember how much you wanted to check one out?"

I could hear Gracie pawing in her stall.

A horn beeped, and I recognized the call of the Yellow Bus. "Barkers are here. Go!"

Catman looked torn, pacing like Gracie had. I guided his long strides toward the barn door. "It's going to be a while, Catman," I assured him. "There are three stages to delivery, and this is just the first. She'll be okay." *Please, God, let her be okay!*

The horn beeped again, and Catman wandered out into the snow in the direction of the van.

"I'm staying." M sat cross-legged on the barn floor.

"No really, M," I pleaded. "Go! Hurry!"

M folded his arms and stayed sitting.

I half expected Dad to barge in at any minute

and drag *me* out. Maybe I'd join M's sit-in. To tell the truth, with Lizzy and Catman gone, the barn seemed too quiet. I didn't know what was about to happen in that stall. I wasn't so sure I wanted to be alone when it did. Eventually I'd call the vet and get him to come for the delivery, but that could still be hours away.

Again came the beep of the Barker Bus.

I trudged out to the van. Dad was leaning in, talking to Mrs. Barker behind the wheel. He looked up when he saw me coming. "Winnie! Are you sure you'll be okay?" He didn't seem mad at me. "Do you want me to stay?"

I couldn't believe he'd asked that. For the first time, Madeline would actually be in church when he looked around for her, and still he'd offered to stay home? "I'm okay, Dad. Thanks though. I'm sorry I can't go. It will probably be hours yet. But Gracie is pacing and—"

"It's okay." Dad opened the back door of the van. "Room for one more?"

"Climb on in!" Mr. Barker called. "Hey, Winnie! Good luck! We'll be praying for you."

I could hear Catman in the back, telling all the little Barkers about Gracie.

"Where's M?" Barker hollered up.

"I guess he decided not to go," I said.

"We'll check in on you when we drop these guys off!" Barker shouted.

I waved, and Mrs. Barker turned the van around by pulling in and out of our driveway. Then she drove away.

Gracie! I rushed back to the barn, where M was still having his sit-in. "You win," I whispered. "We can watch from Nickers' stall if we're quiet. She could put off delivering if she thinks we're watching."

Nickers stood next to the adjoining wall, her head over the divider. She switched her tail and made low, short nickers to Gracie.

I showed M where to peek through the slats. Poor Gracie lay down and got up again—once, twice, a third time. Each time it seemed harder for her to get back on her feet.

A half hour passed. M and I didn't speak, but it wasn't an awkward silence. I was glad he'd stayed with me.

As I watched Gracie jerk her head toward her belly, I could almost feel her pain. Even healthy horses have to go through the pain of giving birth. I prayed she wouldn't suffer, that the foal would be healthy. I hoped.

M sat on the cot and picked up a piece of straw. "Christmas Eve." He turned the straw between his fingers. "Mary, Joseph, the baby." It wasn't a question, but I felt like he was asking something.

"Baby Jesus, yeah." I wondered how much more M really knew about Jesus. "But he didn't stay a baby." It wasn't what I meant to say. I wished Lizzy were here. She could have told M everything just right. Nickers paced, then stuck her head over the stall divider again.

"He always looks like a baby at Christmas," M said. "Like a real kid."

"He was real—*is* real. But he was God too."

"But he was folded up inside his mother." M peeked through the slats at Gracie. I knew what he was thinking. "Why?"

"So he'd know how we feel . . . ," I said, praying I'd get it right. "And then so he could die . . . for us."

"Whoa." M swung around. "I don't get that part."

Help me out here, God. I don't know how to talk about Jesus like this. I can talk to a horse about anything. But people? That's Lizzy's department.

"Well, somebody had to die for our sins—," I

tried, sounding really hoarse. "And it was either him or us."

M didn't say anything, but his eyes were asking.

A picture flashed into my brain, a mind photo I hadn't seen in years—of my mom, Lizzy, and a black stallion. "M, it's different from what Jesus did, but my mom almost died for Lizzy once." He squinted in concentration at me. "Lizzy was little, still crawling. And she was in our yard. But this wild, black stallion my mom was training broke loose and thundered toward Lizzy. I saw it from the window and can still see the exact instant when my mom leaped off the porch and stood right in front of Lizzy as that stallion charged, ears back, teeth bared."

"What happened?" M asked.

"The horse veered off, but he caught Mom's side, and she fell and broke her wrist. But, M, she was willing to die for her baby. And that's what Jesus did, gave up his life for us. Only he had to 'cause of our sins."

Note to self: Never ever give a sermon.

"Whose sins?" M asked.

"Everybody's." Even *you and your kind,* I thought. Even Summer and her kind.

"Sins, huh?" I wasn't sure he'd said it out loud.

"Like lying and stuff."

"Lying . . . ," M repeated, taking another peek at Gracie. "Winnie, there's something I have to tell you, something I—Winnie! She's leaking again!"

I shoved M out of the way and stared through the slats. Water gushed out of Gracie's backside, then a yellowish-brown fluid. "M!" I cried. "Gracie's water's broken!"

M jumped up off the cot. "Fix it!"

*F*ix what?" Catman stood in the stallway, holding Nelson.

"Catman! You're here!" I cried. I thought of a million things at once—*call the vet, get my first-aid kit.*

"Had to be here," Catman said. "Walked back. Cool service though. Gracie cool?"

M had his head pressed to the stall wall, staring in at the mare. Nickers snorted and pawed the ground.

Catman joined us in Nickers' stall. "Did you tell her?"

M didn't answer.

"Do it, man," Catman said. "Or I will."

"Tell her what? Gracie?" *I* had to be the sensible one here. *Think.* "Catman, go inside and call

Dr. Stutzman. Number's right by the phone. M, bring out my first-aid kit. Now!"

Catman left. Gracie curled her lip, pawed, rubbed her tail against the wall. Then I remembered I hadn't told Catman what to say on the phone. I ran after him. Snow fell hard and swirled under the light of a few bright stars. "Catman!" He turned and jogged back to me. "Tell Doc Gracie's water broke, and he needs to get over here fast!"

Catman was staring behind me. M had followed us out. He bent over and moved his finger in the snow, making a loop—a big *U.*

"M!" I shouted. "We don't have time for this!"

He drew another *U* next to the first one. Then he stood up and raised his eyebrows.

"What?" I screamed, so frustrated I wanted to slug both of them.

M leaned over, stuck his head into the now knee-high snow, and stood on his hands.

"Stop it!" I cried. "Why are you—?" I glanced down at M, his head buried in snow up to his shoulders as he stood upside down next to the two *U*'s. *Two U's. Double U's. Upside down . . . Topsy-Turvy-Double-U.* The lines in the snow made a *W.* Upside down, they formed . . . *M!*

"M! You're Topsy-Turvy *W?"* I reached out and shoved his legs, which were sticking up out of the snow.

He toppled backward and bounded to his feet, snow and ice sticking to his head and ponytail.

"How could you do that? And how could you not tell me? I can't believe you—" I wheeled on Catman. "And *you!* You knew all along, didn't you?"

"I wouldn't let him tell," M said, his teeth chattering. "My uncle's horse. He bought her off a guy, thinking he'd sell her for more money. Then he found out she was sick. He swore me to s-secrecy or he wouldn't s-sell her to me. And I was afraid you'd give her b-back."

"I'll go call the vet," Catman said, striding toward the house.

I'd had it with both of them. I turned my back on them and hurried back to Gracie.

M followed me into the barn but kept his distance.

"Did you know she was with foal?" I shouted back.

"Nope," M said. "Uncle Cameron probably would have asked for more money if he'd known. I didn't have another penny."

165

I knew M had sacrificed a lot to buy Gracie. But I wasn't ready to quit being angry. I stormed to the supply room and got my first-aid kit, then waited for Catman to get back.

Gracie squealed, a heart-wrenching cry.

I raced to her stall to see the mare grunting, lying on her side, her legs stiff. She was having contractions. "M!" I yelled. "Get the bandages! Where's Catman!" Even if the vet left this minute, he could miss the birth.

"Can't reach him." Catman startled me. He was standing right behind us.

I wheeled around. "Catman! You *have* to reach him."

"Answering machine said he was at Spidells'. I called the pager, but it didn't work. Called Spidells' and got Summer. She wouldn't get the vet because he was treating her horse—a reaction to a shot or something." Catman panted, out of breath.

I had to act. "M, bring the bandages to Gracie's stall! I'll need water." I slipped in with the mare. It was happening. Gracie was on her feet, and a gray bubble appeared under her tail. The mare's eyes were glazed, and she didn't seem to know I was with her.

"Wow!" Catman peered over the stall door, as M rushed in with clean bandages.

"Catman, I need Doc Stutzman!" I pleaded.

"Chill, Winnie," he said, sounding more like the cool Catman. "I'll get him. On Nickers."

"But—," I started to protest.

"Winnie, help!" M called. "She's falling down."

Catman pulled down Nickers' hackamore, and I ran to Gracie. It did look like she was falling, not lying, down. M tried to ease the landing. I grabbed the bandages and wrapped up her tail as the gray bubble sac broke, and a tiny, bubble-wrapped hoof appeared under the tail, then disappeared again.

Gracie groaned and, with a surge of super-horse energy, struggled to her feet and paced.

"We're off!" Catman shouted.

I looked up in time to see Catman, bareback on my Arabian, trot out of the barn and into the blizzard. Grabbing the jar of Vaseline from my kit, I ran out into the snow after them. I whistled, and Nickers stopped. The wind howled in icy blasts.

As fast as I could I smeared Nickers' hooves with Vaseline. "This should keep her hooves

167

from caking." I hugged my horse, sent them off, and prayed they'd make it—and make it in time.

"Winnie! It's . . . it's waving!"

I raced back into the stall to see one tiny hoof sticking out of Gracie, who was still on her feet. *Please get the other hoof out!* I prayed. "The hooves *have* to come out together!" I cried. "With the foal's muzzle between them, or . . ." I'd heard stories of broken necks, foals being stuck inside mares. If the foal's head was turned back, there'd be nothing we could do. But I'd seen my mom and our old vet deliver a foal that just presented one foot at birth.

"The sleeves, M! Get me the plastic gloves! And smear Vaseline on them!"

I scrubbed my hands with soap and slipped on the plastic sleeves M brought. "I have to help her, fast! You hold her."

I went behind Gracie and reached inside of her until I felt the other hoof. "It's too far back!" I tried to pull it up. Slowly I pushed the right hoof back in just enough so the left hoof could move. "Got it!" I cried, feeling the hoof kick up. "And I feel the nose!"

Gracie snorted, then wobbled and groaned. It was taking everything she had to help her foal.

"Come on, Gracie!" I waited until I felt her push. Then I pulled gently on both hooves. Out they came, and a tiny nose stretched between knobby knees, all wrapped in a clear, sticky sac.

"M! Get back here and help me! Gracie's not going to lie down again. She must know she's not strong enough to do it lying down. You have to catch the foal." In the wild, horses usually deliver foals standing up so they can be ready to defend themselves if they have to. But, even then, foals sometimes break legs, or even necks, when they drop.

"Winnie, is everything—what's—oh—my—!" Dad was stammering from the stallway. Behind him stood Lizzy, Barker, and the entire Barker crew.

"Good Lord, have mercy!" Granny B exclaimed. And it was a prayer that filled the barn.

"Winnie!" Lizzy shouted.

"Winnie, honey!" Mrs. Barker cried, holding back a couple of her sons. Mr. Barker and Barker took care of the others. "Can we do anything?" she asked.

Mason tried to run over to us, but Madeline caught him. "Do you want us to leave, Winnie?" she asked.

But I couldn't answer. Gracie let out a squeal and a grunt, and the foal slid out and straight into M's open arms.

Nickers whinnied.

"Yea!" Lizzy yelled, but somebody shushed her.

Gracie's knees buckled, and she slid to the ground and onto her side. I was rushing to her when M hollered, "Winnie! It's not breathing!"

I heard Lizzy gasp. Somebody prayed.

I grabbed a clean towel and knelt in front of the foal. Heavy mucous clung to its nose and face. I wiped frantically with the towel, trying to clear the nostrils.

Nothing. Still no breathing.

"Lay her down, M!" I screamed. "Rub her all over!"

A towel flew into the stall. "Did you see the towel, Winnie?" Dad called.

"Got it!" M cried, rubbing the tiny foal's chest.

Please, God. Please!

At that instant, Nickers cantered into the barn, and Catman jumped off. "Dr. Stutzman's coming!" I heard a car door slam outside.

And I got an idea. Horses are nose breathers.

"Catman!" I shouted. "Get me that anti-freeze/turkey baster!"

"What?" Madeline asked.

Catman, covered in snow, ran into Gracie's stall with the baster.

"Go help M!" I said, taking the baster, squeezing it, and sticking it into the foal's nostril. I released the suction ball and heard slurping as the mucous was drawn out.

"It moved!" Catman cried, on his knees beside M, both rubbing furiously.

I used the baster on the other nostril. The foal sneezed. The eyes blinked. She breathed. She was a little filly, and she was breathing.

Thank you, God. Tears made my eyes blur as I stared at the miracle in front of me.

All around us cheers broke out. I looked at Catman and M and figured I'd never seen either of them smile that big or look that happy.

Then, as suddenly as the cheer had begun, it stopped.

Gracie, flat on her side, lifted her head and craned her neck around to see her baby. But she was too weak. I went to her and held her head so she could see the tiny foal at her feet. "You did it, Gracie! She's okay!" Tears were streaming down my face, landing on sweet Gracie.

Then she closed her eyes, laid her head in my lap, and stopped breathing.

I felt an arm on my shoulder. Then someone else lifted Gracie's head. Someone lifted me to my feet. I felt, more than saw, Lizzy, Dad, and Catman around me, guiding me out of Gracie's stall.

"You did an amazing job, Winnie." It was Dr. Stutzman. "No vet could have done better. It's a miracle that filly survived!" He whispered to Dad. "I heard . . . sorry . . . didn't know . . . came as soon as I heard." Then he whispered more, but everything started spinning and my whole body turned to water.

I didn't faint, but I came close. Dad made me sit in the stallway until my head cleared. The Barkers left quietly, while Lizzy and Dad sat next to me.

Dad squeezed my hand.

"The foal needs colostrum!" I struggled to get to my feet. "She should get most of it in the first hour!"

"I'll get it!" Lizzy jumped up. "You wait right there!"

"Gracie—" I felt sick inside. And I knew I'd always carry that picture of her as she strained to see the foal she'd sacrificed her life for.

"Tell M and Catman to move the foal in with Nickers," I said.

Dad got up. And in seconds, M came out, carrying a perky, beautiful foal with bright eyes, curly black hair, four white stockings, and a blaze down the middle of the cutest face I'd ever seen. He carried her in to Nickers, who walked right to the foal and began sniffing her and nickering.

I slipped back in with Gracie. I had to see her one more time, to tell her good-bye. She looked beautiful and peaceful. "Thanks, Gracie," I whispered. Her dapple-gray coat looked almost white. I knelt down and scratched her chest.

Dr. Stutzman came into the stall. "Why don't you let me do my job, Winnie? I can't tell you how sorry I am that I didn't get here sooner." He took my elbow and guided me out of the stall. "But I couldn't have done anything for that mare you didn't do. I'm going to take care of her now, though, and take her away for you. It's the least I can do. I'll go make arrangements now. If you need any help feeding that colos- trum, I'll be right back."

Dad walked Doc to his truck, and Lizzy came back with a thawed bag of colostrum. Catman poured six ounces into one of the bottles.

"Foals can only absorb the antibodies in this stuff for about 12 hours," I explained, taking the bottle. I was going to fight for this foal as hard as Gracie had. "Most of the antibodies get absorbed in the first hour or two. We better get on it."

The foal was half lying, half sitting, her long legs tucked under her, and her neck held high. She was gorgeous. And so was Nickers, who licked the foal's ears and cheek, acting like a mother. I was so proud of her.

I knelt beside the foal, shook drops of the milk on my fingers, and put my fingers to her mouth. She licked the milk. Her raspy tongue made me shiver. I shook out more milk and let her lick that too. Then I put my arm around her neck and held the bottle with the nipple facing my wrist, higher than her nose. The foal stretched her neck like she would have for an udder. She took the nipple and drank.

"Far out!" Catman whispered.

"Ditto," M said.

The foal's mouth slipped off the nipple, and she looked around, taking in Nickers, the stall, the two strange guys watching her every move. Then she turned back to me. After three or four start-and-stops, she'd finished half of the colostrum in the bottle.

I let her take a break, and I went over to Catman and M.

"Totally keen," Catman said.

I could almost see a wave of sadness pass over M's face. "Gracie did it," he said, his voice soft. "She gave up her life for her foal." He looked right at me, and I knew he was saying a lot more, understanding a lot more.

It was past midnight. And there we were, in a stable, watching a miracle. "Merry Christmas," I whispered.

Dad and Lizzy watched with us as the foal tried to stand up. First she stuck out her long legs and sat like a dog. Nickers walked circles around her. The foal lunged forward, then fell back.

Lizzy burst into giggles.

Again the foal lunged forward, off her back legs, until she stood, wobbly, legs spread wide, nose to the ground.

"Good for you!" Dad cheered.

She moved one stockinged leg forward, then another, then sprawled down again.

Watching the foal made me think of Dad and me, of God and me. I'd fallen down a lot lately. But nobody was giving up on me. And thinking about how everybody had pulled together tonight—well, there wasn't anybody I'd rather be with than *me and my kind*.

Nickers walked beside the foal, her head lowered over the foal's back.

"It's not so bad being an orphan," M said quietly. "Not when great people adopt you."

I knew M was adopted. I'd met his parents. He was right.

I fed the foal the rest of the bottle. Then Dad convinced me to go in the house and get warmed up before the next feeding. Catman and M stayed in the barn, and Lizzy, Dad, and I traipsed through the snow under the bright North Star and a sliver of a moon.

Mason was sitting on the floor, staring at the Christmas tree when we walked inside.

Madeline brought us hot chocolate after we shed our coats. "Mason and I decided nobody would be getting any sleep tonight." She glanced at her watch. "Make that *this morning*. So we vote that we all celebrate right now."

"Sweet!" Lizzy cried, dashing to her bedroom and coming out with an armload of gifts.

We laughed through the whole gift exchange. Catman had left presents for all of us under the tree. And every present was a roll of wrapping paper.

Madeline passed out self-opening gifts, her invention. "You just pull the ribbon, and the paper automatically comes off. Then the box flops open!" Mason and I got body sleds. They looked like snow pants with wide skis sewn inside.

"My latest invention!" Madeline exclaimed. "You can't lose them like you could a sled."

Dad got Madeline a "neck saddle." He fastened it onto her shoulders and hoisted Mason up. "See? Fun for Mason, and easier on your back!"

Lizzy passed out painted rocks to all of us, each rock a creation. "Most of them have verses," she said, putting one wrapped rock back under the tree. "Except Catman's. I painted the peace sign on one side. The other side says *I won't take you for granite!* Won't Mr. Coolidge love it!"

I opened my rock from Lizzy and read what she'd written in tiny, neat white letters: *Thank God for his Son—a gift too wonderful for words!* — 2 Corinthians 9:15.

"Thanks, Lizzy. I love it!" I wished I could have pulled out the terrarium, complete with the greatest iguana in the world for her.

Finally I opened the gift from Hawk. "It's a horse-angel pin," I whispered. It might have been one of those flying Pegasus horses. But all I saw was a horse angel. I pinned it on and phoned Hawk. She was glad to hear from me, even though I woke her up.

"You haven't opened the present from me yet, Winnie," Dad said when I came back out to the living room. He handed me a box wrapped in Sunday comics.

I opened it. Inside was a beautiful blue halter, perfect for a perfect colt. I couldn't believe my dad had bought it. "But . . . but you kept saying . . ."

Dad sat down on the couch with me. "I know. I went overboard, didn't I? I just didn't want to see you get hurt again." I knew he was thinking about Mom like I was. "But I was hoping too, Winnie."

"I feel so bad," I said. "You all got me great gifts, and I didn't get you anything."

Mason was sitting on the floor, staring at his Lizzy rock. Lizzy and Madeline stopped what they were doing and walked over to us.

"Are you kidding, Winnie?" Lizzy cried. "What you did out there in that barn, that cute little colt getting born! That was the best gift I've ever seen!"

"Lizzy's right," Madeline said, smoothing Mason's hair. "I'm not sure how Mason will handle all of this when he understands more . . . about Gracie. But I wouldn't have missed that birth for all the patents in D.C.! Right, Mason?"

Mason was still staring at the rock. He acted as if he hadn't heard her.

I wondered if he understood, if he knew he'd never see Gracie again. He seemed to be slipping into that secret place of his. I pictured him hugging Gracie's leg, staring at her dappled hair, touching her belly where the baby horse was sleeping. And in that instant I knew what I needed to do.

"Would everybody come out in the barn with me?" I asked.

"Now?" Madeline said.

I filled another bottle with colostrum. Then everybody followed me back to the barn. M, Catman, and Nickers were faithfully watching over the foal.

"M!" Lizzy cried. "What did you do?"

The foal was wearing M's black sweatshirt, which was a great idea and a great fit.

"Thought she looked cold," he said.

Mason wandered to Gracie's stall and stared in. The stall was empty now. Dr. Stutzman had taken care of that. But Mason looked like he still felt the absence of another horse he'd loved and lost.

Madeline tried to pull him away, but he shook her off.

I went over to him. "Mason," I said, "I want you to meet somebody who needs your help."

He turned his blank face to me.

I glanced up at Madeline. "He'll be okay."

I carried Mason into Nickers' stall and felt his body surge with energy and life again the second he caught sight of the foal.

"Baby horse!" he cried, squirming out of my arms and stumbling to the foal.

I showed him how to hold the bottle and

feed her. He giggled, but held on to the bottle with both hands.

"Jack," I heard Madeline say to Dad, "I don't know if I want him to go through this all over again."

I stood up beside Mason, my heart pounding and calming at the same time. I glanced at M, and his eyes told me we were thinking the same thing. He knew what I had to do.

"It's okay, Madeline. You don't have to worry. The foal isn't going anywhere." I turned to Mason. "She's yours, Mason. The baby horse belongs to you."

Somebody gasped.

Mason squealed and hugged the foal.

I turned to Madeline. "We'll keep her for you free. And I'll train her and do all the work." I knelt and put one arm around the foal and the other around Mason. "But this foal is yours to keep, Mason."

It should have been about the hardest thing I'd ever done. I'd loved Gracie, and I loved her foal every bit as much. But somehow, loving the foal and loving Mason . . . the only thing left to do was give them to each other. "Merry Christmas, Mason."

We were still hugging and crying and laughing when Barker walked into the barn, carrying a bleating, white goat. Behind him came Mr. Barker, with Mark and Matthew, each carrying two puppies.

"Merry Christmas!" Mr. Barker shouted.

"Eddy Barker!" Lizzy exclaimed. "Where did you get that?"

"Granny. She had it brought up from her farm. Granny claims goats' milk is the closest thing to horses' milk. She thought this nanny might come in handy."

"Your granny is amazing, Barker!" I cried. And she was right about the milk. Once the foal got enough colostrum, I could get her to nurse from the goat. "Tell her thanks, Barker."

Barker struggled with the goat and fought to keep his balance. Catman, trailed by a swarm of cats, came to the rescue. The two of them carried the goat into an empty stall and shut the door.

M met Mark and Matthew in the stallway, and Matthew handed him the two black puppies he was carrying. The puppies licked M's face and wagged their tails. Then Mark handed him one of the two dogs he was carrying.

"Hope your parents like their Christmas gifts,"

Mark said, clinging to the remaining dog in his arms. "I liked your idea of giving yourself a puppy. So I gave me Zorro."

"It was our compromise," Mr. Barker added. "Mark gets to keep the runt of the litter, and he'll still be able to visit M's three dogs."

The whole time Mason had held his ground with the foal, making sure that she kept coming back to the bottle.

Snow fell lightly as dawn glowed through the barn windows. We could have all been sealed inside one of those snow globes. I thought about Mary and Joseph and Jesus as a baby. We had Nickers, a foal, a goat, puppies, and cats instead of a donkey, sheep, and camels. But Jesus, not the baby, was in our barn too. And as I watched Mason holding that bottle while the foal tugged life from it, I could almost hear angels sing.

We'd all seen the miracle, how something so humble in a stable could suffer to bring us a gift—free and priceless grace. Gracie *had* been a gift horse.

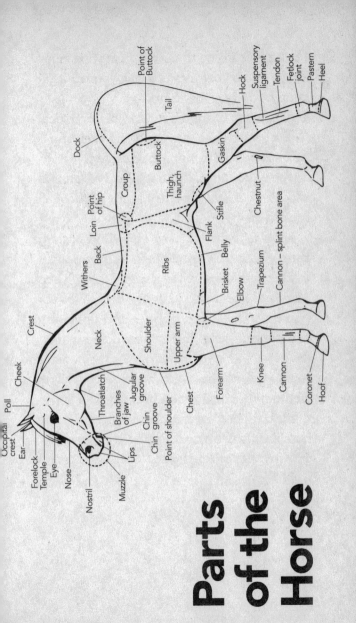

Parts of the Horse

Horse Talk!

Horses communicate with one another . . . and with us, if we learn to read their cues. Here are some of the main ways a horse talks:

Whinny—A loud, long horse call that can be heard from a half mile away. Horses often whinny back and forth.
Possible translations: *Is that you over there? Hello! I'm over here! See me? I heard you! What's going on?*

Neigh—To most horse people, a neigh is the same as a whinny. Some people call any vocalization from a horse a neigh.

Nicker—The friendliest horse greeting in the world. A nicker is a low sound made in the throat, sometimes rumbling. Horses use it as a warm greeting for another horse or a trusted person. A horse owner might hear a nicker at feeding time.
Possible translations: *Welcome back! Good to see you. I missed you. Hey there! Come on over. Got anything good to eat?*

Snort—This sounds like your snort, only much louder and more fluttering. It's a hard exhale, with the air being forced out through the nostrils.

Possible translations: *Look out! Something's wrong out there! Yikes! What's that?*

Blow—Usually one huge exhale, like a snort, but in a large burst of wind.

Possible translations: *What's going on? Things aren't so bad. Such is life.*

Squeal—This high-pitched cry that sounds a bit like a scream can be heard a hundred yards away.

Possible translations: *Don't you dare! Stop it! I'm warning you! I've had it—I mean it! That hurts!*

Grunts, groans, sighs, sniffs—Horses make a variety of sounds. Some grunts and groans mean nothing more than boredom. Others are natural outgrowths of exercise.

*****

Horses also communicate without making a sound. You'll need to observe each horse and tune in to the individual translations, but here are some possible versions of nonverbal horse talk:

EARS
Flat back ears—When a horse pins back its ears, pay attention and beware! If the ears go back slightly, the

horse may just be irritated. The closer the ears are pressed back to the skull, the angrier the horse.

Possible translations: I don't like that buzzing fly. You're making me mad! I'm warning you! You try that, and I'll make you wish you hadn't!

Pricked forward, stiff ears—Ears stiffly forward usually mean a horse is on the alert. Something ahead has captured its attention.

Possible translations: What's that? Did you hear that? I want to know what that is! Forward ears may also say, I'm cool and proud of it!

Relaxed, loosely forward ears—When a horse is content, listening to sounds all around, ears relax, tilting loosely forward.

Possible translations: It's a fine day, not too bad at all. Nothin' new out here.

Uneven ears—When a horse swivels one ear up and one ear back, it's just paying attention to the surroundings.

Possible translations: Sigh. So, anything interesting going on yet?

Stiff, twitching ears—If a horse twitches stiff ears, flicking them fast (in combination with overall body tension), be on guard! This horse may be terrified and ready to bolt.

Possible translations: Yikes! I'm outta here! Run for the hills!

Airplane ears—Ears lopped to the sides usually means the horse is bored or tired.
Possible translations: *Nothing ever happens around here. So, what's next already? Bor-ing.*

Droopy ears—When a horse's ears sag and droop to the sides, it may just be sleepy, or it might be in pain.
Possible translations: *Yawn . . . I am so sleepy. I could sure use some shut-eye. I don't feel so good. It really hurts.*

TAIL

Tail switches hard and fast—An intensely angry horse will switch its tail hard enough to hurt anyone foolhardy enough to stand within striking distance. The tail flies side to side and maybe up and down as well.
Possible translations: *I've had it, I tell you! Enough is enough! Stand back and get out of my way!*

Tail held high—A horse who holds its tail high may be proud to be a horse!
Possible translations: *Get a load of me! Hey! Look how gorgeous I am! I'm so amazing that I just may hightail it out of here!*

Clamped-down tail—Fear can make a horse clamp its tail to its rump.
Possible translations: *I don't like this; it's scary. What are they going to do to me? Can't somebody help me?*

Pointed tail swat—One sharp, well-aimed swat of the tail could mean something hurts there.

Possible translations: *Ouch! That hurts! Got that pesky fly.*

OTHER SIGNALS

Pay attention to other body language. Stamping a hoof may mean impatience or eagerness to get going. A rear hoof raised slightly off the ground might be a sign of irritation. The same hoof raised, but relaxed, may signal sleepiness. When a horse is angry, the muscles tense, back stiffens, and the eyes flash, showing extra white of the eyeballs. One anxious horse may balk, standing stone still and stiff legged. Another horse just as anxious may dance sideways or paw the ground. A horse in pain might swing its head backward toward the pain, toss its head, shiver, or try to rub or nibble the sore spot. Sick horses tend to lower their heads and look dull, listless, and unresponsive.

As you attempt to communicate with your horse and understand what he or she is saying, remember that different horses may use the same sound or signal, but mean different things. One horse may flatten her ears in anger, while another horse lays back his ears to listen to a rider. Each horse has his or her own language, and it's up to you to understand.

🐎 Horse-O-Pedia

Akhal Teke—A small, compact horse with an elegant head. The Akhal Teke, also known as Turkmen, is fast, strong, and reliable—a great, all-around riding horse.

American Saddlebred (or American Saddle Horse)—A showy breed of horse with five gaits (walk, trot, canter, and two extras). They are usually high-spirited, often high-strung; mainly seen in horse shows.

Andalusian—A breed of horse originating in Spain, strong and striking in appearance. They have been used in dressage, as parade horses, in the bullring, and even for herding cattle.

Appaloosa—Horse with mottled skin and a pattern of spots, such as a solid white or brown with oblong, dark spots behind the withers. They're usually good all-around horses.

Arabian—Believed to be the oldest breed or one of the oldest. Arabians are thought by many to be the most beautiful of all horses. They are characterized by a small head, large eyes, refined build, silky mane and tail, and often high spirits.

Barb—North African desert horse.

Bay—A horse with a mahogany or deep brown to reddish-brown color and a black mane and tail.

Blind-age—Without revealing age.

Brumby—A bony, Roman-nosed Australian scrub horse, disagreeable and hard to train.

Buck—To thrust out the back legs, kicking off the ground.

Buckskin—Tan or grayish-yellow-colored horse with black mane and tail.

Camargue—A tough, surefooted, but high-stepping and beautiful horse native to southern France. Camargues have inspired artists and poets down through the centuries.

Cannon—The bone in a horse's leg that runs from the knee to the fetlock.

Canter—A rolling-gait with a three time pace slower than a gallop. The rhythm falls with the right hind foot, then the left hind and right fore simultaneously, then the left fore followed by a period of suspension when all feet are off the ground.

Cattle-pony stop—Sudden, sliding stop with drastically bent haunches and rear legs; the type of stop a cutting, or cowboy, horse might make to round up cattle.

Chestnut—A horse with a coat colored golden yellow to dark brown, sometimes the color of bays, but with same-color mane and tail.

Cloverleaf—The three-cornered racing pattern followed in many barrel races; so named because the circles around each barrel resemble the three petals on a clover leaf.

Clydesdale—A very large and heavy draft breed. Clydesdales have been used for many kinds of work, from towing barges along canals, to plowing fields, to hauling heavy loads in wagons.

Colic—A digestive disorder in horses, accompanied by severe abdominal pain.

Colostrum—First milk. The first milk that comes from a mare containes the antibodies the foal needs to prevent disease.

Conformation—The overall structure of a horse; the way his parts fit together. Good conformation in a horse means that horse is solidly built, with straight legs and well-proportioned features.

Crop—A small whip sometimes used by riders.

Cross-ties—Two straps coming from opposite walls of the stallway. They hook onto a horse's halter for easier grooming.

Curb—A single-bar bit with a curve in the middle and shanks and a curb chain to provide leverage in a horse's mouth.

Dapple—A color effect that looks splotchy. A dapple-gray horse will be light gray covered with rings of darker gray.

D ring—The D-shaped, metal ring on the side of a horse's halter.

Dutch Friesian—A stocky, large European breed of horses who have characteristically bushy manes.

English Riding—The style of riding English or Eastern or Saddle Seat, on a flat saddle that's lighter and leaner than a Western saddle. English riding is seen in three-gaited and five-gaited Saddle Horse classes in horse shows. In competition, the rider posts at the trot and wears a formal riding habit.

Founder—A condition, also known as laminitis, in which the hoof becomes deformed due to poor blood circulation. Major causes are getting too much of spring's first grass, overeating, drinking cold water immediately after exercise, excessive stress, or other ailments.

Frog—The soft, V-shaped section on the underside of a horse's hoof.

Gait—Set manner in which a horse moves. Horses have four natural gaits: the walk, the trot or jog, the canter or lope, and the gallop. Other gaits have been learned or are characteristic to certain breeds: pace, amble, slow gait, rack, running walk, etc.

Galvayne's Groove—The groove on the surface of a horse's upper incisor. The length of the Galvayne's groove is a good way to determine a horse's age.

Gelding—An altered male horse.

Hackamore—A bridle with no bit, often used for training Western horses.

Hackney—A high-stepping harness horse driven in showrings. Hackneys used to pull carriages in everyday life.

Halter—Basic device of straps or rope fitting around a horse's head and behind the ears. Halters are used to lead or tie up a horse.

Hay Net—A net or open bag that can be filled with hay

and hung in a stall. Hay nets provide an alternate method of feeding hay to horses.

Headshy—Touchy around the head. Horses that are headshy may jerk their heads away when someone attempts to stroke their heads or to bridle them.

Heaves—A disease that makes it hard for the horse to breathe. Heaves in horses is similar to asthma in humans.

Hippotherapy—A specialty area of therapeutic horse riding that has been used to help patients with neurological disorders, movement dysfunctions, and other disabilities. Hippotherapy is a medical treatment given by a specially trained physical therapist.

Horse Therapy—A form of treatment where the patient is encouraged to form a partnership with the therapy horse.

Hunter—A horse used primarily for hunt riding. Hunter is a type, not a distinct breed. Many hunters are bred in Ireland, Britain, and the U.S.

Leadrope—A rope with a hook on one end to attach to a horse's halter for leading or tying the horse.

Leads—The act of a horse galloping in such a way as to balance his body, leading with one side or the other. In a *right lead*, the right foreleg leaves the ground last and seems to reach out farther. In a *left lead*, the horse reaches out farther with the left foreleg, usually when galloping counterclockwise.

Lipizzaner—Strong, stately horse used in the famous Spanish Riding School of Vienna. Lipizzaners are born black and turn gray or white.

Lunge line (longe line)—A very long lead line or rope, used for exercising a horse from the ground. A hook at one end of the line is attached to the horse's halter, and the horse is encouraged to move in a circle around the handler.

Lusitano—Large, agile, noble breed of horse from Portugal. They're known as the mounts of bullfighters.

Manipur—A pony bred in Manipur, India. Descended from the wild Mongolian horse, the Manipur was the original polo pony.

Mare—Female horse.

Maremmano—A classical Greek warhorse descended from sixteenth-century Spain. It was the preferred mount of the Italian cowboy.

Martingale—A strap run from the girth, between a horse's forelegs, and up to the reins or noseband of the bridle. The martingale restricts a horse's head movements.

Morgan—A compact, solidly built breed of horse with muscular shoulders. Morgans are usually reliable, trustworthy horses.

Mustang—Originally, a small, hardy Spanish horse turned loose in the wilds. Mustangs still run wild in protected parts of the U.S. They are suspicious of humans, tough, hard to train, but quick and able horses.

Paddock—Fenced area near a stable or barn; smaller than a pasture. It's often used for training and working horses.

Paint—A spotted horse with Quarter Horse or Thoroughbred bloodlines. The American Paint Horse Association registers only those horses with Paint, Quarter Horse, or Thoroughbred registration papers.

Palomino—Cream-colored or golden horse with a silver or white mane and tail.

Palouse—Native American people who inhabited the Washington–Oregon area. They were hightly skilled in horse training and are credited with developing the Appaloosas.

Percheron—A heavy, hardy breed of horse with a good disposition. Percherons have been used as elegant draft horses, pulling royal coaches. They've also been good workhorses on farms. Thousands of Percherons from America served as warhorses during World War I.

Peruvian Paso—A smooth and steady horse with a weird gait that's kind of like swimming. *Paso* means "step"; the Peruvian Paso can step out at 16 MPH without giving the rider a bumpy ride.

Pinto—Spotted horse, brown and white or black and white. Refers only to color. The Pinto Horse Association registers any spotted horse or pony.

Poll—The highest part of a horse's head, right between the ears.

Post—A riding technique in English horsemanship. The rider posts to a rising trot, lifting slightly out of the saddle and back down, in coordination with the horse's bounciest gait, the trot.

Presentation—The way the foal comes out at birth. Normal presentation is for a foal to have two front hooves appear, followed by the nose between the legs.

Przewalski—Perhaps the oldest breed of primitive horse. Also known as the Mongolian Wild Horse, the

Przewalski Horse looks primitive, with a large head and a short, broad body.

Quarter Horse—A muscular "cowboy" horse reminiscent of the Old West. The Quarter Horse got its name from the fact that it can outrun other horses over the quarter mile. Quarter Horses are usually easygoing and good-natured.

Quirt—A short-handled rawhide whip sometimes used by riders.

Rear—To suddenly lift both front legs into the air and stand only on the back legs.

Roan—The color of a horse when white hairs mix with the basic coat of black, brown, chestnut, or gray.

Snaffle—A single bar bit, often jointed, or "broken" in the middle, with no shank. Snaffle bits are generally considered less punishing than curbed bits.

Sorrel—Used to describe a horse that's reddish (usually reddish-brown) in color.

Spur—A short metal spike or spiked wheel that straps to the heel of a rider's boots. Spurs are used to urge the horse on faster.

Stallion—An unaltered male horse.

Standardbred—A breed of horse heavier than the

Thoroughbred, but similar in type. Standardbreds have a calm temperament and are used in harness racing.

Stifle—The joint of a horse's hind leg. The stifle works somewhat like the knee in humans.

Surcingle—A type of cinch used to hold a saddle, blanket, or a pack to a horse. The surcingle looks like a wide belt.

Tack—Horse equipment (saddles, bridles, halters, etc.).

Tennessee Walker—A gaited horse, with a running walk—half walk and half trot. Tennessee Walking Horses are generally steady and reliable, very comfortable to ride.

Thoroughbred—The fastest breed of horse in the world, they are used as racing horses. Thoroughbreds are often high-strung.

Thrush—An infection in the V-shaped frog of a horse's foot. Thrush can be caused by a horse's standing in a dirty stall or wet pasture.

Tie short—Tying the rope with little or no slack to prevent movement from the horse.

Trakehner—Strong, dependable, agile horse that can do it all—show, dressage, jump, harness.

Turnout time—

Time a horse spends outside a barn or stable, "turned out" to exercise or roam in a pasture.

Twitch—A device some horsemen use to make a horse go where it doesn't want to go. A rope noose loops around the upper lip. The loop is attached to what looks like a bat, and the bat is twisted, tightening the noose around the horse's muzzle until he gives in.

Waxing—The formation of thick drops of first milk that begin leaking from a mare's udders. It may look like honey or wax.

Welsh Cob—A breed of pony brought to the U.S. from the United Kingdom. Welsh Cobs are great all-around ponies.

Western Riding—The style of riding as cowboys of the Old West rode, as ranchers have ridden, with a traditional Western saddle, heavy, deep-seated, with a raised saddle horn. Trail riding and pleasure riding are generally Western; more relaxed than English riding.

Wind sucking—The bad, and often dangerous, habit of some stabled horses to chew on fence or stall wood and suck in air.

🐎 Author Talk

Dandi Daley Mackall grew up riding horses, taking her first solo bareback ride when she was three. Her best friends were Sugar, a Pinto; Misty, probably a Morgan; and Towaco, an Appaloosa; along with Ash Bill, a Quarter Horse; Rocket, a buckskin; Angel, the colt; Butch, anybody's guess; Lancer and Cindy, American Saddlebreds; and Moby, a white Quarter Horse. Dandi and husband, Joe; daughters, Jen and Katy; and son, Dan (when forced) enjoy riding Cheyenne, their Paint. Dandi has written books for all ages, including Little Blessings books, Degrees of Guilt: *Kyra's Story*, Degrees of Betrayal: *Sierra's Story, Love Rules,* and *Maggie's Story*. Her books (about 400 titles) have sold more than 4 million copies. She writes and rides from rural Ohio.

Visit Dandi at www.dandibooks.com

Starlight Animal Rescue

A new series by Dandi Daley Mackall

🐾   🐾   🐾   🐾   🐾   🐾

Not so far away from Winnie and Nickers is an amazing place called
Starlight Animal Rescue, headed by none other than Catman's cousin,
who frequently e-mails the Pet Help Line and Winnie for horse-gentling
tips. The rescue is a farm where hopeless horses are loved and trained,
where discarded dogs become heroes, where stray cats are transformed
into trusted companions, and where troubled teens find help through
the animals they rescue.

A sneak peek at Book 1, *Runaway* . . .

I've run away seven times—

never once to anything, just away from.

Maybe that's why they call me a "runaway"

and not a "run-to."

Meet Dakota Brown, who used to love all things "horse" until she lost
everything, including hope. The minute she sets foot in the Starlight
Animal Rescue, she plans her escape. But can an "impossible" horse
named Blackfire and this odd collection of quirky animal lovers be the
home she's always dreamed of?

Winnie
The Horse Gentler

1 **WILD THING**

2 **EAGER STAR**

3 **BOLD BEAUTY**

4 **MIDNIGHT MYSTERY**

5 **UNHAPPY APPY**

6 **GIFT HORSE**

7 **FRIENDLY FOAL**

8 **BUCKSKIN BANDIT**

COLLECT ALL EIGHT BOOKS!

Can't get enough of Winnie? Visit her Web site to read more about Winnie and her friends plus all about their horses.

IT'S ALL ON WINNIETHEHORSEGENTLER.COM

There are so many fun and cool things to do on Winnie's Web site; here are just a few:

★ PAT'S PETS

Post your favorite photo of your pet and tell us a fun story about them

★ ASK WINNIE

Here's your chance to ask Winnie questions about your horse

✦ MANE ATTRACTION

Meet Dandi and her horse, Chestnut!

★ THE BARNYARD

Here's your chance to share your thoughts with others

✦ AND MUCH MORE!